The Alibi

by

Marilyn Baron

The Alibi

Cover Art by *Debbie Taylor*

The Wild Rose Press, Inc.
PO Box 708
Adams Basin, NY 14410-0708
Visit us at www.thewildrosepress.com

Publishing History
First Mainstream Historical Rose Edition, 2017
Print ISBN 978-1-5092-1611-6
Digital ISBN 978-1-5092-1612-3

Published in the United States of America

Dedication

My working title for this novel was "My Year In Prison" because it was sparked by my imagination after the time I spent as an Information Specialist for the Florida Department of Corrections soon after I graduated college. From my first day on the job—when there was an escape from the women's correctional institution—to my last, my time there was action-packed and prepared me with the skills I'd need for the rest of my career.

Tear tracks stained his face. Blood stained his white T-shirt. His eyes were glazed over. He appeared to be in shock. He looked like hell.

"Director, are you all right?"

He didn't answer.

"Director Baintree," I shouted, "are you hurt?" My raised voice blew him out of his stupor and back into battle mode.

"What the hell does it look like? No, I'm *not* all right. I need you to take me home."

"Where's Miss Braddock? Does she need a ride somewhere?"

"Miss Braddock?" The director appeared confused.

"Savannah Braddock. The woman who lives here."

"She's gone," he said simply, deflated, his face crumpling.

I don't know what prompted me to do this, but I walked around him and ran from room to room. There weren't many places to look in that tiny apartment. Apparently, all it needed were the basic necessities—a kitchenette, a bathroom, and of course, a bedroom. That's where I found her, half naked, sprawled out on the bedspread, a pool of blood soaking the white eyelet duvet cover. And the handle of an oversized kitchen knife sticking out of her abdomen.

I wanted to scream, but no sound came out. I began hyperventilating. I was going to be sick—I knew I wouldn't make it into the bathroom.

"For God's sake, stop." The director walked into the bedroom. He rounded on me, and my breathing calmed, but I continued to stand there, immobilized, staring at the once perfect, now bloody and lifeless body of Savannah Braddock.

Praise for Marilyn Baron and...

STUMBLE STONES
"Modern characters find themselves thrown into a mystery that spans generations, and to discover the answers, they have to look to the past. Marilyn Baron perfectly blends that laugh-out-loud humor of a new romance with the heartbreaking story of a family torn apart by the Holocaust. Touching and beautifully written with marvelous attention to setting and history."

~Jennifer Moore, author of Change of Heart

~*~

"Marilyn Baron brings a unique style to her quirky and fast-paced stories that keeps readers turning pages."

~New York Times Bestseller Dianna Love

~*~

UNDER THE MOON GATE
"A surefire blockbuster...a treasure trove of mystery and intrigue. It sparkles with romance."

~Andrew Kirby

"Historical romance at its best."

~TripFiction

Prologue

When I read about the director's tragic death on the Internet, I ran into my home office and took out a dusty, laminated ID card from a desk drawer I hadn't opened for years, not since I'd left the prison system. I blew off the dust and detritus and examined my picture. Was that really me? I looked pretty good there all those years ago. So fresh and hopeful and thin! Then the world was full of possibilities.

That was before all the secrets and lies, secrets I'd hoped to take to the grave. Secrets I had kept, until now. Secrets that informed my life and all the decisions I'd made up until this point, from where I lived to who I'd marry. And I'm the worst about keeping secrets, as my kids like to remind me.

But now the director was dead, killed in the crash of the small plane he was piloting, along with his wife, Miss Julia.

What is that expression, *Dead people can't tell tales*? Maybe it was time for the truth to come out. The truth I'd kept bottled up inside me for years. The truth about the brutal death of Judge Savannah Braddock, still an unsolved case, as far as I could tell. I'd never told anyone about it or the part I'd played in the cover-up. And not a day in my life went by that I didn't see her partially clothed, beautiful but bloody body lying there on the bed and think about what had happened that morning.

The director's glowing obituary spoke of lower recidivism rates and prevention and his department's stellar institutional and community-based programs to foster academic and vocational education, to assist offenders by providing substance abuse prevention services and other support services such as transitional housing. Willard Ware Baintree was credited with many of the cutting edge programs of the day.

The article speculated about the director's sudden, unexplained retirement from the Department at the height of his career, but they couldn't have guessed the reason. Only three living people knew the real reason, and I was one of them. They reported, rightfully, that the director was a visionary. But they left out one important fact. The illustrious, much beloved, and universally revered Willard Ware Baintree, one-time head of the criminal justice system in Florida, was himself a criminal.

I sank into my seat. Swiveling in my office chair, I couldn't help but travel back to my first day on the job, and the first time I'd met Willard Ware Baintree.

Chapter One

I wasn't alone in that first meeting with the director. My future direct boss, Peggy Springer, was also there. I'd soon learn that Peggy was never very far from the director's side. Whatever the director needed, Peggy would make it happen.

The director was an imposing man, standing or sitting—tall and lanky, with a sturdy body and a killer tan on a face that made me want to reach out and touch it. Blond, broad-shouldered, one could even say handsome, for a middle-aged man, he had a definite commanding presence. He was the kind of man who was used to issuing orders he expected people to follow. So I could understand why Peggy Springer, and every other woman in the Florida correction system— not many in those days—were under his spell. Talk was that one woman in particular, Judge Savannah Braddock, was having a torrid affair with the director.

Peggy was a hyperactive chain smoker who didn't believe in delegating, because, I soon found out, she believed no one could do the job better than she could. She was like the original Energizer Bunny combined with Speedy Gonzalez on steroids, a spinning top that never stopped, a hummingbird too busy fluttering to light, and a Category Five super storm headed on a collision course for the coast.

Peggy was phenomenal in an emergency, forceful

and quick on her feet. I could learn a lot from her. And I wanted to. In contrast to my fairly low-key personality, Hurricane Peggy was totally overwhelming, not to mention domineering, but she generously took me under her wing and immediately commanded my loyalty.

Peggy knew a lot about loyalty. She worshipped at the feet of the director of the Division of Corrections, Willard Ware Baintree, of the landmark Supreme Court case, *Wiggins v. Baintree* that had something to do with defendants' rights. The case my boyfriend, Daniel Krantz, was currently studying in his Criminal Procedure class (which he called Crim Pro) in law school at the University of Virginia, the first stop on his way to a prestigious law firm to follow his dream of becoming a partner. A dream that apparently no longer included me.

Daniel and I had dated seriously throughout college, but while all of my girlfriends were getting married or engaged, I was trying to find a job. Were we still together? That was unclear. What *was* clear was that he was impressed when I told him I had interviewed for my first job out of college with *the* Willard Ware Baintree. I actually sat across the table from the director a few weeks after I graduated college.

Daniel predicted I would never get a job in public relations in the current economic climate. I was determined to put my college education to good use and to prove him wrong. He wasn't saying anything my father hadn't said. My dad had encouraged me to go into teaching, one of the only ways a woman could really make a living.

I majored in public relations and minored in

criminology. My senior project had been working with a task force of citizens in Alachua County, trying to convince the voters to approve the funds to build a new jail. When I found out Daniel had been accepted to law school at UVa, without even asking me if I wanted to marry him, which I did, I found myself at a crossroads. I didn't want to live with my parents. I wanted to spread my wings and find a job in my field.

Which is how I found myself sitting across the desk from Willard Ware Baintree, a criminal justice superstar, appointed by the governor after having served as warden of a state correctional institution for fifteen years.

Willard Ware Baintree was the head of the prison system back when a prison was still a prison and not a correctional institution. When a guard was still a guard and not a correctional officer. A warden was still a warden and not a superintendent. And a prisoner was still a prisoner and not an inmate. During my first year in the prison system, under Director Baintree's reign, things would change dramatically, to more politically correct terminology. The Division of Corrections would eventually become the Department of Offender Rehabilitation. And the director would become the Secretary. Peggy would work for the Office of the Secretary in the Office of Communications and was eventually promoted to Director of Public Affairs. Now I understand they've come full circle and are calling it the Florida Department of Corrections (FDC) and that the new Secretary is a woman. And if that don't beat all, as they would say in the South.

"Merritt," the director began the interview, fastening his gaze on my legs, which in those days were encased in stockings and actually worth looking at. I tugged the short hemline of my dress down as far as it would go, which wasn't very far, and wished I could adjust my girdle. Was my dress too short? Or too tight? Was I showing too much cleavage? It was the only dress I owned. I'd lived in jeans the past four years.

I was just a Jewish girl from Miami. What did I know about criminal justice? Only that when my mother used to tease her friends about their matzoh ball soup, she would say, "You should taste Shirley's matzoh balls. They're hard as a rock, not light and fluffy like mine. It's *criminal* what that woman does to those matzoh balls."

At the Division of Corrections, the director was next to God. I thought I should genuflect, but what was the proper way for a Jewish girl to recite the Trinitarian formula? In Nomine *Potroast* et Filii et Spiritus Sancti?

The director cleared his throat. "Why do you want to work for the Division of Corrections?"

My palms were sweaty. My throat was parched. There was no bottled water back then. This man was going to decide my fate, my future, my career.

Why did I want to take a job with the biggest good-old-boy network in the state? And why did I want to live in the middle of nowhere? Because a job was a job. We were in the middle of a recession, and there weren't that many jobs in journalism or PR. The state was a stable employer, and at the time, the prison system was Florida's largest state agency. I had college loans and a car loan to pay off, and I needed to support myself. Because, back then, I had no plan. I wasn't engaged, and I had no idea whatsoever what I was going to do with the rest of my life. I had nowhere else to go unless

I wanted to move back to Miami and move in with my parents. Somehow I didn't think that was the answer he was looking for. I had majored in PR and wanted a career in my profession, so if not now, *cuándo?* as they say in Miami. Should I cite statistics about recidivism? He had probably forgotten more than I'd ever learned in college about the subject.

So I explained to him about my senior project and showed him the work product from the campaign in a thick black binder—the press releases, news clippings, recommendations from the task force, and the end product, communicating that we had succeeded in getting the county to supply the funds to build a new jail.

He seemed suitably impressed, and within the week, I had accepted a job as an Information Specialist I. I was in. Little did I know what I was in for.

So I got in my jade green Thunderbird with the white leather roof, which I was still paying off monthly, and headed for Watertown, Florida.

Watertown was located between Tallahassee and Florida State Prison, home of the electric chair, otherwise known as Old Sparky.

The infamous Old Sparky was built in 1923 to carry out executions. Executions had ceased in 1964, and resumed in Florida in 1979 as a result of a Supreme Court overturning its ruling and upholding the constitutionality of the death penalty. I've since heard that they built a new electric chair made of oak and that the only thing new about the current electric chair is the wooden structure of the chair itself. The apparatus that administers the electric current to the condemned prisoner is the same as the one used for years, and I've been assured it is regularly tested to ensure proper functioning. I doubt whether the inmates waiting on Death Row cared about the new "farm style" look of the chair's outer structure.

When the director took over, he convinced the legislature to move his headquarters to unincorporated Watertown to be closer to the correctional pulse and the prison population. And closer, rumor had it, to Savannah Braddock.

Watertown was a misnomer, because there wasn't a body of water anywhere in sight. I soon learned Watertown was in the middle of Downtown Nowhere, the dictionary definition of a sleepy town—a town that was practically in a coma—where the Spanish Moss grew thick and the Southern accents thicker.

Watertown, which wasn't even officially a town, was inappropriately advertised as the "Best Town on Earth," with some less than stellar eating establishments lining the wide parkway that led up to the courthouse square. Sprawled along the road were Sandra's Beauty Nook, Fenster's Hardware, Shelley's Seafood, Watertown Bed and Breakfast, and Pizza Napoli. I hadn't been to many towns outside of Miami, but that slogan seemed like either deceptive advertising or the most hopeful attempt to, as they say in the South, put lipstick on a pig. I couldn't imagine spending the rest of my life in Watertown. Still, we were in the middle of a recession, and I was happy to have a job.

When I got the job at the prison system, I endured the expected incarceration jokes.

"How long are you in for?" my father asked.

"Why does the prison system need Public Relations?" my mother wondered.

"So should I tell my friends that my girlfriend is doing time in the Big House?" Daniel teased.

No matter how many times I told them I was doing PR, not time, I continued to be teased mercilessly.

Like every journalism major, I had visions of writing the Great American Novel. Mine would be entitled "My Year in Prison." Which meant I had to stay on the job for at least a year. Just enough time for my next employer to see that I had staying power. A sense of commitment. A trait my boyfriend was definitely lacking. It turns out I could have written a blockbuster about what I'd seen there. But, as I said, I was determined to carry my secrets to the grave, so my blockbuster exposé never materialized.

Chapter Two

Peggy swore me to secrecy when we stopped by Savannah Braddock's apartment on my first day on the job. Our purpose was to pick up the director in DC 1, the license plate of the premiere white car in the division motor pool fleet. We were driving him to the women's correctional institution nearby. Four female prisoners had escaped, and the director, being a hands-on leader, like Peggy, wanted to make his presence known on the scene.

"We'll catch them soon," Peggy assured me from the driver's seat, as we watched the tender moment between the director and Savannah play out on the doorstep. "Most escapees are found within four miles of the prison, still in their orange jumpsuits. Or on their way to the house of a family member."

When the couple came out of the apartment, Savannah was wearing a filmy white silk negligee that showed off her generous curves and more than a hint of breast. She was leaning suggestively into him, then entwined herself around him, kissing him with a hunger that was almost palpable, and certainly embarrassing.

I found myself wondering: Did Savannah call him "Willi" in private when they were in the throes of passion? He tried to disentangle himself from her grasp a number of times, but she clung to his body as if it were a lifeline, and by the look of regret fastened on his finely chiseled face, it was obvious he would have preferred to crawl back into bed, *her* bed. Her honey-blonde hair was half in, half out of curlers. Which told me she was confident enough in his interest that she could be herself. It gave her a disheveled look. Curlers or no, she was a classic beauty, in the mold of Marilyn Monroe. It would have been a domestic scene but for the fact that the director was married and not, I later found out, to Savannah Braddock.

"Is this where the director lives?" I asked Peggy, surprised that such an illustrious man lived in such an unremarkable apartment. "I heard he was pretty wealthy."

"His wife is the wealthy one," Peggy explained. "The director was a beat cop when she met him. Actually, he started out doing lawn work for her family. She married him, put him through college and law school, and has been devoted to promoting his career ever since. Her family has a lot of power in the Florida Panhandle and throughout the state. She has her eye on the governor's mansion. She's a guiding influence, but the success is all his. He's earned every bit of it. The man is brilliant. He has a mind like a steel trap. So no, he doesn't live here. He does spend quite a lot of time here. Sleeps over whenever he can."

I had never seen a steel trap, but I didn't think it hurt that the director could charm the skin off a snake. "Then why are we picking him up here?"

Peggy looked like she'd rather chew glass than answer my question.

"The director (she always called him that, so I got into the habit of calling him that too) had an emergency meeting with the judge."

I nodded like I understood, but I didn't.

"Who is she?" I nodded toward the apartment doorway.

"The Honorable Savannah Braddock, the youngest judge on the second judicial circuit court," Peggy answered simply, pursing her lips and slanting her eyebrows. In her current state of undress, Savannah Braddock looked less than honorable. Nevertheless, the message was clear. This tryst would remain between us.

Was this a love nest? Did the director pay the rent on the place? Did he often meet in *bedchambers* with this particular judge? Did he know what she wore underneath her robes? These were questions I was dying to ask but couldn't. Wouldn't dare. Not on my first day on the job. My lips were sealed.

Peggy needn't have worried. Who was I going to tell? These were the days before Facebook, before Twitter, before Instagram, before the Internet. Before Amazon knew what you were thinking before you even thought it.

Despite the lack of instant digital communications, Peggy was tuned into everything that was going on in the division. Information was currency, and as the director's eyes and ears, she capitalized on it. She went drinking with one or more of the regional directors, the CFO, Deputy Director of Institutions, Facilities Management Director, Comptroller, Legislative Affairs director or the Chief of Staff every night like she was just one of the guys. She could drink them under the table, and she had all the dirt on everyone. She was all about secrets and not above trading in them. As just one of the boys, she was whip smart and good at her job, so she commanded their respect.

Peggy wasn't married, wasn't dating anyone, that I knew about, so her entire life was devoted to the director and keeping him informed and happy. Not that it would come to that, but infidelity aside, I was convinced she would take a bullet for him. Come to his defense even if he murdered someone, even if that murder was captured on some kind of recording device—these days, a cell phone, which at that time wouldn't be in widespread use for another fifteen years.

And further, judging from the look of longing in my boss's eyes, I intuited that Peggy would have traded places with Savannah Braddock in an instant, even though she was young enough to be his daughter. Savannah Braddock wasn't much older. But apparently, Peggy Springer wasn't the director's preferred body type. She was short-waisted and boxy, with a black pixie-like pageboy and severe eyebrows she wrestled with that almost met in the middle. Rumor was that the director went more for the blonde bombshell type, a type that Savannah Braddock embodied perfectly. I was blonde and some would say shapely, but Savannah's curves put mine to shame.

Savannah Braddock's meteoric rise through the ranks of the good-old-boy network was astonishing, the way Peggy told it. The story went that the director met her at a reception after he addressed a young lawyer's group. Using his influence and connections, he got her a prestigious clerking job with a judge in Tallahassee. Within a few years, she received an interim appointment as a judge in neighboring Watertown, which was unusual for such an inexperienced attorney. Not that she didn't have a good head on her shoulders. But the talk was that it was her assets below the shoulders that prompted that appointment. Of course, there was plenty of tongue-wagging about how she got there, capitalizing on the unique type of experience she did have, but the wagging was never in front of the director.

Their affair was the worst-kept secret in the Division, along the lines of a reported affair between a certain U.S. President and a popular movie screen actress. Savannah Braddock was the director's Marilyn. He was besotted with her. He was probably in love with her. What man wouldn't be? But he was too much of a gentleman and he had too much to lose to leave his wife, Miss Julia, Peggy confided. That was simply not done. This was the South, after all, and men had their standards. Not to mention Miss Julia was from the Rawlins family, the most prominent and wealthy family in North Florida. And the director owed everything he had and everything he was in the world to her.

The first time I heard the series of clicks of the locking mechanisms that shut the metal gate behind me at the entrance to the maximum security women's prison, I was startled, but Peggy assured me I'd get used to it. Peggy had written out a statement for us to read to the media when they called the temporary press room she had arranged to be set up at the prison. And she was right. The inmates were found later that afternoon, not far from the prison grounds, still in their prison garb. And in those days, orange was definitely not the new black.

In the meantime, I got my trial by fire, answering reporter questions about the four women. What were their names? How old were they? What were they serving time for? Did they have husbands? Children?

How much time was left in their sentences? How did they escape? How much time would be added to their sentence for their escape attempt? My first day on the job was exciting. I wondered what the rest of the days would bring.

Chapter Three

The next time I saw Savannah Braddock was at the director's annual Fourth of July party that he and his wife hosted at their sprawling ranch on the outskirts of town.

I had just arrived, and I looked around for Peggy because she was the only person I really knew. It was no surprise that I spotted her in a tight-knit circle—mostly a coil of men, all department heads and close friends of the director—around Savannah Braddock. I wondered if they were there for her protection or for the purpose of hiding her from their boss's wife. They looked like the palace guard. I knew the director ran his division like General Patton and these were his trusted lieutenants. Or were these men also interested in Miss Braddock but didn't realize she was already taken by their boss? That was unlikely. Everyone in the division knew everything. Everyone knew there was an invisible stamp on Savannah's forehead that read Property of the Director.

Rumors spread like kudzu—who was sleeping with whom, who was up for a promotion, who was the boss's favorite. These men and Peggy were all jockeying for position.

I walked up and tapped Peggy on the shoulder. She turned and smiled at me like she was actually happy to see me.

"Wow, this is some place," I said, admiring the sprawling ranch and the antebellum home. "How many acres do you suppose it is?"

Peggy spread out her arms, indicating that the ranch spread into infinity. "The Baintrees own the land as far as you can see, including all the cattle and horses. There's a horse whisperer they have set up in the corral, if you want a demonstration. They're offering hayrides, and they can saddle horses, if you can ride."

This was the closest I'd ever come to a horse.

"Mrs. Baintree just redecorated, and she's giving tours of the house."

"I'd love to get a look at the place," I said. "Where's the director?"

She pointed toward the verandah. The director stood next to an older woman in a plain-looking dress, her angular face topped by white hair pulled back in a bun.

"Is that the director's mother?"

Peggy laughed. "That's his wife, Miss Julia. A lot of people make that mistake."

The contrast between Mrs. Baintree and Savannah Braddock, with her movie-star looks and snug-fitting sundress waging a losing battle to contain her curves, couldn't be more pronounced.

"She's—I mean, there's a big difference between, er, what I mean is…"

"I was shocked the first time I met her, too," Peggy interrupted. "This was Miss Julia's family's farm, and the house has been in her family for generations. The director is devoted to her and their two daughters."

I didn't need Peggy to identify the daughters. They looked exactly like their mother, right down to their plain faces and frumpy fashion statements.

I frowned. How devoted could the director be to his family in light of his frequent assignations with his mistress? I mean, I didn't really know for sure how frequent, but judging from the one time I'd seen them, I doubted it was a one-time fling.

"Does she know that—?" I tilted my head in Mrs. Baintree's direction.

"Of course not," Peggy hissed. "This is not the place to talk about it."

I glanced at Mrs. Baintree, who looked like a librarian in her unflattering shift dress. Her eyes were flashing daggers in Savannah's direction. Peggy was mistaken. This woman knew all about her husband's mistress, and she was furious that he was flaunting her at their party. You'd have to be a blind fool not to see it. But when it came to the director, Peggy was a blind fool.

I thought it best not to mention the director's infidelity again. What kind of arrangement did the director have with his wife? Was their marriage in name only? Did they still love each other? What made the director stray?

"They lead separate lives," said Peggy. "They don't have the same interests. She has her female friends. They're more into fundraising for local causes, the battered women's shelter, adult literacy, animal rescue. He likes to hunt and fish and camp. And, of course, fly. He has a private plane he pilots."

From everything I'd heard about Savannah Braddock, she was the director's hunting buddy, fishing buddy, camping buddy, and bedmate, and she could outshoot any man. As far as I could tell, she wasn't a woman who particularly needed protecting, though from the way she was acting around the men, she could dissemble with the best of them.

I kept an eye on the two of them—Savannah and the director—and couldn't help but notice the passionate looks they shot each other. Those looks flew like electric sparks; they simmered like the sun bleeding through the horizon. At one point, he sauntered over to her with a plate of food.

"You eat yet, Savannah?" I heard him whisper. "I fixed you a plate." Their fingers brushed as she took the plate from him. "Thank you, *Director*," she practically purred in her sexy Southern accent. "I was getting awfully hungry." He laughed, and she surreptitiously touched her hand to his thigh. "This was just what I needed, Willi." Ha, ha. I was right. She did call him Willi. They whispered a few private words to each other, probably about when they would hook up later on.

I felt sorry for Mrs. Baintree. She might have money and prestige and her husband's name, but she no longer had his heart. She was dowdy but looked harmless enough.

Well, who was I to judge? My boyfriend was three states away, and he hadn't called me in a week. Was I supposed to wait for him, or spend the rest of my life in Watertown? Not that I didn't like my job, but I knew I could never live here on a permanent basis. And what other options did I have? Looking around, I couldn't see myself with any of these men. Did I want to become the wife of a prison guard or even a superintendent? Almost all of the men in the director's inner circle were married, if that meant anything anymore.

The director was hot, in a Joe Don Baker sort of way, ripped and powerful, but too old for me, and anyway, his eyes could hardly tear themselves away from Savannah.

"I shouldn't be too long, honey," the director whispered. "Wait up for me, now, all right?"

Savannah pouted. "You know I will. Should I get one of these big strong, handsome gentlemen to take me home?" She rubbed her forefinger over her bottom lip and then sucked on it.

The director frowned. He intuited her meaning. She was trying to make him jealous, and it was working.

A hand shot up. It was Roy Starnes, the comptroller, one of the only single men in the group, who was practically salivating and had been monopolizing Savannah's attention since I'd arrived. "I'll—" he offered. The director cut him off abruptly mid-sentence.

"Peggy, honey, you won't mind taking Miss Braddock on home for me, now would you?"

Roy sulked and flexed his fingers into a fist. The director had embarrassed him again. Not only in front of his colleagues but in front of Savannah. Everyone knew he had a crush on Savannah and that he didn't approve of his boss's indiscretion. Peggy practically saluted and assured him she wouldn't mind at all. *Way to pimp out your boss, Peggy.*

The director trusted the men, but only to a point. Savannah was his, but she got restless when he wasn't around. The men seemed to genuinely like him, but they weren't above being jealous—of his home, his stature, and most of all, the unattainable Savannah.

"I'll see you later, then," Savannah whispered.

"Don't be too long, now, Willi."

The director could hardly contain his impatience. And from the looks of his erection, painfully visible through his tight jeans, it was obvious he wanted to make his exit now and jump right into Savannah's bed, but since he was the host, he had to keep up appearances for his guests and possibly his wife.

To make his point, he addressed Roy in front of the crowd. "Roy, give me a few minutes and then come get me about that emergency situation—you know the one?"

Roy's face flushed. Not only had he become a yes-man but he was aiding and abetting what he thought was a sin, to his Christian sensibilities. I imagined he'd been hoping to get Savannah alone and rescue her from her predicament, whether she wanted to be rescued or not. To teach her that there was a better way. A way Savannah Braddock was definitely not interested in.

The director flashed a lazy smile and looked back at Savannah, who grinned like a woman who had her man just where she wanted him. A woman who was adored. By the director and every other man in her line of sight.

Chapter Four

In those days, the Public Affairs Office consisted of a small group. In addition to Peggy and me, there was Stanley, an Information Specialist II, who had been a reporter for the *Tallahassee Leader*, and our secretary, Jean, an attractive middle-aged woman who was married to the owner of a successful real estate firm in town.

Stanley was a hard-bitten journalist with sagging, sallow skin and jowls and a lazy eye. With his short stature, he resembled a wise old gnome. He looked like he was perpetually craving a smoke, but he'd apparently kicked the habit. Stanley looked beaten down, like the type of guy who was going to be here for the rest of his career. No ambition. At least he had left behind the low-paying, long hours of working for a newspaper. But he was industrious and kind, willing to offer me, the new kid on the team, the benefit of his experience.

It was only the dawn of the computer age, so we all worked on electric IBM Selectric typewriters. My primary job was to write press releases, answer reporters' questions when Peggy and Stanley were not available, and edit the *Correctional Courier*, the official newsletter of the Florida Division of Corrections, which was distributed to all division staff throughout the state and which we around the office affectionately referred to as "The Clink." We covered stories about staff, training programs, and inmate news and features.

I also wrote articles for such publications as the *Sheriff's Star*. My best article was about a reformed inmate who had been arrested for dealing drugs but who now counseled kids to stay away from drugs. Unfortunately, the day my article appeared in the magazine, on the front cover, no less, I learned that the man had been rearrested for dealing drugs. That should have come as no surprise. Drug offenses accounted for most prison admissions.

Over the course of my year in the system, I visited a number of prisons—from major correctional institutions to re-entry centers, work camps, forestry camps, and road prisons, as well as training facilities and community release centers. The first time I went to supervise the printing of the newsletter, I drove four hours to Sumter Correctional Institution, which housed the printing press, operated by the inmates.

When I walked into the institution, the superintendant took me into his office and laid his gun on the table. I assumed it was loaded. From his office, I had a perfect view of the entire complex through his picture window. "You see those gun turrets around the perimeter of the prison? If something goes wrong, they're the only ones who can protect you. I can't carry a gun into the prison because I might be overpowered. So if someone attacks us, run. There's nothing I can do to save you." Then he led me into the lion's den, where the printing press sat along with the convicts running it.

He dropped me off in the area with the printing press and introduced me to the foreman and his team. The foreman was a big man with a range of tattoos, and he already had my job on the press. I'll call him Hulk. He tore off the front sheet. The colors were a little off. To me, the publication looked too red, but I wasn't going to say anything to Hulk. Who knew what would happen if I criticized his work? But he was good at his job and took pride in his product. He could tell I was less than sure of myself, so he made adjustments until he got the color the way *he* wanted it. I stayed for about four hours to re-proof the job and make sure there were no additional corrections, and until he was satisfied and the job rolled off the press. He would ship the trimmed newsletters back to the Central Office for mailing once they were dried, scored, and trimmed. But I did take some sample sheets with me. I was pretty proud of my first newsletter. And I was grateful to Hulk. Looking back, that was where I learned the art of working with printers. Printers liked me because I rarely complained. If I could work with dangerous inmates, I could work with any printer.

My first non-emergency assignment was to cover the Quincy Correctional Institution Cooking School graduation. Originally a vocational center, the cooking school was created to teach culinary skills to inmates. These men, who had little or no hope of getting out, who had spent most of their careers murdering or causing disturbances and riots, starting fires, or trying to escape, were trained in cooking to staff the various institutions throughout the state. They learned to make fried chicken, cakes, and various desserts.

I drove to Quincy, which was only about twenty-five miles away. After I entered the gate and parked near the facility, I walked up to the receptionist.

"I'm looking for a man named Jack Basin."

"Oh, you want the Sink or the Tub," she said. I didn't really want to know why they called him that. Did he drown someone in the sink or stab someone in the shower?

At that moment, a large black man walked toward me. A large black man wielding a bowie knife. The kind of survival knife Crocodile Dundee carried when he exclaimed, "That's not a knife," and whipped out his own blade while adding, "That's a knife."

"Um, hello, Mr. Sink, er, Mr. Basin. I'm Merritt Saxe from the Division newspaper. I'd like to ask you a few questions."

I recovered my cool when I learned that he, the graduate, was carrying the knife in preparation for slicing into a large sheet cake for the ceremony.

Like my mother, you might be curious as to what a PR person for the prison system does. How can you improve the image of the prison system? You'd be surprised. Given the fact that most of the inmates who serve time in prison will eventually be free, the agency focused on equipping its offenders with the tools they would need to become productive citizens when they were released.

We had a lot to be proud of and many positive stories to tell. We were hiring more women, minorities, and people with disabilities, and improving staff training. The director traveled all over the country looking for innovative ideas to implement in his system. There were the special inmate re-entry programs, such as the inmate beekeeping program, which trained soon-to-be-released inmates to maintain a colony of honey bees and collect honey. The same with the Second Chance Farm, a horse program that trained inmates to rehabilitate thoroughbred racehorses for use by the Division of Corrections and other law enforcement agencies and qualified the graduates to go to work in the industry as groomers and stable managers. Then there was an inmate dog adoption program that was a partnership program between the Division and various community rescue groups and animal service agencies to increase the adoptability of shelter dogs.

It was up to me to come up with appealing headlines for the programs, such as "Inmate Beekeeping Program: A Honey of an Idea" and "Second Chance Farms: We're Not Horsing Around" or "Inmate Dog Training Program: Barking up the Right Tree."

But the meat and potatoes of my job was cranking out a steady stream of DC assault and escape advisories, issued whenever a correctional officer or probation officer was attacked by an inmate in the line of duty. It typically went like this:

Dateline—Chipley, Fla., or Clermont, Fla., or Sneads, Fla., (Insert Name of appropriate Florida city).

On (DATE), a correctional officer was assaulted by an inmate at the (Insert Institution Name).

Inmate (Insert Name) (Insert Inmate ID Number) attacked the correctional officer (Insert Name) at approximately (Insert Time) with a (Insert Method of assault—shard of PVC pipe or other homemade weapon—kicked an officer in the leg or head-butted said officer in the chest while being escorted from the shower, or bit an officer.) [The options were endless and exponential.] *Staff responded and took appropriate action until the inmate became compliant.* [I wasn't sure what that action entailed or what they meant by compliant.] *Medical staff examined the officer involved. Inmate X or Y or Z will receive a disciplinary report for this assault. The Office of Inspector General will investigate this incident.*

Not too difficult once I got the formula down.

Of course, inmates continued to escape, and we continued to churn out Inmate Escape Alerts:

Dateline. The Florida Division of Corrections is aggressively searching for escaped inmate (Insert Name) (Insert Inmate ID Number) on (Insert Day of the week, date and time). Inmate X was serving a five-year prison sentence for (manufacturing heroin and trafficking in stolen property). We believe the inmate may be in (Insert Name of County). Florida Division of Corrections dog-tracking teams and search teams are working with local law enforcement, but we are also asking for your help in finding this inmate.

Usually the escapees were minimum custody inmates who worked outside the fence of a prison.

During my tenure at the Division, the number of inmates increased 127 percent. As a result, the director got the inspired idea to ease the overcrowding by housing the inmates in tents. Tent City was Director Baintree's brain child, as were most of the innovative ideas. The system was overflowing, and we had no place to put the inmates, so we arranged to house them in tents for months. That was perhaps the most newsworthy event ever reported on. The story took off, and we got media inquiries from reporters from all over the world and frequent visits to the unique temporary housing project.

The publicity called attention to our plight and

caused the legislature to fork over some much-needed dollars to fund new buildings. Just in time, too, because winter was knocking at the door, and the inmates couldn't have survived the weather conditions outside. The three of us were pumping out press releases about Tent City, and Peggy cut and pasted articles about Tent City in a scrapbook that she kept in a bureau in her office…and proudly showed anybody who walked by.

When I started with the Division, tents were commonplace, but by the end of my tenure, the courts intervened, claiming that as the weather grew colder and the potential for hurricanes and other storms became a concern, inmates could not be kept in such living conditions. The public wasn't too happy about the tent cities either, since they were rightly concerned about escapes.

Stanley and I worked hard but never as hard as Peggy. She worked day and night, it seemed. She never took a vacation. Never took time off even to go to the doctor. The director relied on Peggy to keep his secrets and do his bidding and, many times, be his driver. If I hadn't witnessed the emotion between the director and his mistress with my own eyes, I might have thought there was something untoward about how close he was with his public affairs manager. The director was having his own public affair, which, as I already pointed out, everyone in the Division (with the possible exception of his wife) seemed to know about. Peggy always needed to be accessible to the director. Until one day she wasn't, and I had to step up to the plate. That's when everything went disastrously wrong.

Peggy's telephone line was ringing. Last night at the barbecue she had confided to me that she had a gynecology appointment for a minor procedure she'd been putting off for months. She was in so much pain that finally she had no choice. She said she'd be back the following morning. She hated to leave the office in our charge. She was an overseer, a real micromanager. Nothing got out or got by without her approval.

"Now, if the director asks for me, tell him I'm meeting with a reporter. Don't tell him where I am, for God's sake."

Got it. You wouldn't want him to know you have female problems, since you've done such a great job convincing him you're one of the boys. She was obviously uncomfortable discussing her female issues with her boss. Men didn't have excessive vaginal bleeding or cysts on their ovaries, or whatever she was having checked out. It had to be pretty bad for her to leave the office in our care. She was probably advised to stay at home for a week after the procedure, but Peggy was Superwoman. The normal rules of recuperation didn't apply to her.

"Nothing is going to happen in one day," I assured her. I had never been so wrong about anything in my life. In fact, I was dead wrong.

Chapter Five

Not ten minutes after Peggy walked out the door, her line began ringing insistently, and it wouldn't stop. I was the only one in the office, so I answered it, in case it was important. I hoped it wasn't a reporter. Worse, it was the director. I wasn't completely comfortable dealing with him yet. He was larger than life. The truth was, he frightened me.

He was short and gruff. "I need Peggy."

I blew out a breath. *Okay, let's just dispense with the niceties.*

"Uh, um," I sputtered. What a wuss. I was acting like a complete idiot. I needed to handle this like a professional. My boss was counting on me.

"Peggy isn't here at the moment." *How's that for professional?*

"Where the hell is she? Dammit, I need her!"

Whoa, Nelly! What the heck was wrong?

"I-Is there anything I c-can d-do for you?" I offered. It was the last thing in the world I wanted to do. In fact, I wanted to be anywhere but in this office, answering my boss's phone. I prayed that he'd call back tomorrow when Peggy returned.

"Can I take a message?"

"I don't need a receptionist," he said abruptly. "I need Peggy. Who is this?"

"It's Merritt Saxe, sir."

"Peggy's new girl," he said.

Actually, I'm an Information Specialist I, thank you very much. Crap, he wasn't asking for my title.

"Okay. Listen to me, Miss Saxe. I need you to get on over here right away."

I held my stomach. "W-where is here, sir?" I asked.

"To Miss Braddock's. You and Peggy were here to pick me up, remember? It's, uh, 393 Magnolia Lane in the, uh, Creekside Apartments. Apartment 201. How fast can you get here?"

"I'll get in the car right now and—"

"Don't take a fleet car, ya hear? This has nothing to do with company business."

"Do you want me to bring anything?"

"Bring anything? This ain't a picnic, Miss Saxe. Just bring yourself and get the hell over here as fast as you can. And don't tell anybody where you're going."

Yowser! From his angry tone, I could tell something was seriously wrong. What was he going to ask me to do? I would usually bring a pad of paper or a notebook to a meeting. Did he want me to cover a story? And what did Savannah Braddock have to do with it?

I switched the office phones over to the answering machine. Why did Stanley and Jean have to take lunch at the same time? Peggy would kill us if she knew the Public Affairs office was uncovered. I had to bet she was safely under anesthesia and wouldn't call in.

My stomach was cramping, but I'd better be up to the task, whatever it was.

I drove as fast as I could, within the speed limit, trying to recall where the Creekside Apartments were.

Not far from the office, just a few blocks, and I was there. Which apartment did he say? Was it 201? Or 102? I hoped I'd recognize it from my last visit, but they all looked alike. I was trying to figure out what to say to the director. I didn't want to appear a tongue-tied amateur.

I got out of the car and walked up the stairs to Number 201. Hesitating, to collect my thoughts and catch my breath, I knocked once, lightly, and then again more forcefully. The director opened the door and pulled me in without ceremony.

Tear tracks stained his face. Blood stained his white T-shirt. His eyes were glazed over. He appeared to be in shock. He looked like hell.

"Director, are you all right?"

He didn't answer.

"Director Baintree," I shouted, "are you hurt?" My raised voice blew him out of his stupor and back into battle mode.

"What the hell does it look like? No, I'm *not* all right. I need you to take me home."

"Where's Miss Braddock? Does she need a ride somewhere?"

"Miss Braddock?" The director appeared confused.

"Savannah Braddock. The woman who lives here."

"She's gone," he said simply, deflated, his face crumpling.

I don't know what prompted me to do this, but I walked around him and ran from room to room. There weren't many places to look in that tiny apartment. Apparently, all it needed were the basic necessities—a kitchenette, a bathroom, and of course, a bedroom. That's where I found her, half naked, sprawled out on the bedspread, a pool of blood soaking the white eyelet duvet cover. And the handle of an oversized kitchen knife sticking out of her abdomen.

I wanted to scream, but no sound came out. I began hyperventilating. I was going to be sick—I knew I wouldn't make it into the bathroom.

"For God's sake, stop." The director walked into the bedroom. He rounded on me, and my breathing calmed, but I continued to stand there, immobilized, staring at the once perfect, now bloody and lifeless body of Savannah Braddock.

"We've got to get out of here, now," he ordered.

I took a deep breath to stave off my sickness.

"D-did you c-call 9-1-1?" I asked.

"No. I can't be seen here. Someone will find her. I'll make sure of it."

"Are you sure she's—" I couldn't bring myself to say the word. But I knew, just from looking at her, her pale face and the stiffness of her body, that she was. And I was just as sure that the director had killed her. He certainly had the strength to overpower her and stab her with enough force to kill her. It hadn't been an easy death. She had bled out. The director had had an assignation with her after the barbecue last night and had undoubtedly slept over, which Peggy admitted he often did. So he had opportunity. But what was his motive? Had she been threatening to go public or to go to his wife? Was *she* having an affair? Who else would find her? She was pretty much off limits to anyone but the director. Did she even have any female friends who were concerned about her? A family? I guess they'd miss her in court. But was this her permanent residence or just an illicit meeting place? Did anybody else but

Peggy and me know about this little hideaway?

I looked around the room. A picture of Savannah and the director lay under smashed glass on the floor. Shaking out the jagged glass cautiously, I grabbed the frame and the picture and tucked it into my purse.

The director looked at the picture and nodded. Suddenly he surfaced from shock and went into control mode. He grabbed my arm and started pulling me out of the bedroom.

"Merritt, we need to go, now. That's an order." And just like that, I was inducted into the director's cadre of people who lived to do his bidding and to protect him. I was doing what I was certain Peggy would have done, what she would have wanted me to do.

I wanted to ask the most obvious question, but if he could kill the woman he loved with such brute force, what could he do to me? This was the man everyone revered as someone who upheld the law. And he had broken it in the worst way imaginable.

Trembling, I grabbed a white terrycloth robe from the vanity chair on the way out. It was a woman's robe, Savannah's robe. But she wouldn't be needing it anymore. The director couldn't walk out of the apartment in a blood-soaked T-shirt.

I thrust the robe toward him. "Here, put this on." He obeyed. And that was the first of many steps I took in aiding and abetting a murderer. Apparently, protecting a killer was part of my job description now. I wondered how many crimes Peggy had covered up for him.

I helped the director slip into the front passenger seat, his hands folded as if he were already strapped into a straightjacket or the electric chair. I wondered how long he would last in the general prison population. Not even a day. Would he eventually go to Florida State Prison for a date with Old Sparky? And how would he feel to be incarcerated in his own prison system?

I emptied my stomach on the grass next to my new car and wiped off the vomit with my shirtsleeve. I started the engine. "Are you sure you want to go home? What about your wife?"

I was talking to him like I was in his inner circle, which I wasn't. I hardly knew him. I was talking to him like I was calm and collected, but I was definitely not.

"My wife and daughters have gone to visit her mother in Jacksonville. No one's home. I appreciate you doing this. That was smart thinking back there, picking up that picture."

A day ago, kudos from the director might have had me walking on air. Today, I didn't know how to feel. Did he expect me to tell Peggy? Did he want me to? I had to tell someone. How could I keep a secret like this?

"What about your car? We can't just leave it here."

"Good thinking. I'll get one of the boys to come pick it up. Just get me home."

As I got closer to the director's ranch, he began talking but kept his eyes on the road.

"Is there anything you want to ask me?"

I gave him a sidelong glance. Yeah, there were a million questions going through my head. I had my opening, but I couldn't form the words.

"If you want to know if I killed her, I didn't. I loved her."

I bit the inside of my cheek, drawing blood. Did I believe him? Who else could have done this?

"I'm going to get cleaned up, and I want you to call my secretary and tell her to clear my schedule. I'll be working from home for the rest of the day. You'll be working with me on a special project. A project we've been working on since early this morning."

It took me a second to realize what he was saying. He needed me to be his alibi. How would that look, for me to be working at the director's house? I didn't report to him. I didn't have any special skills that someone in his inner sanctum couldn't offer. I never thought I'd see him again after that first interview. I later found out that the director interviewed everyone who worked for him. From his tone, I gathered refusing wasn't an option.

"Do you really want me to work at your house?"

"No," he barked. "But don't go back to the office. Go home, take the rest of the day off. I don't care where you go. Do we have an understanding?" His eyes locked onto mine as I pulled around the circular driveway that curved around his stately home and dropped the director off at his front door.

I felt threatened, but what could I say? I nodded.

"I won't forget this," he called out.

Neither will I. Not ever.

"Sorry about the blood in your car."

I looked at the vacant seat where he'd been and reminded myself to try to clean the blood off the white leather seats when I got back to my apartment.

As I pulled away, the door opened, and I caught a glimpse of Miss Julia. She collapsed into his arms, and he closed the door behind them.

The director had said Miss Julia was with their

children in Jacksonville. Maybe she had come home early. Maybe he'd called her home for help. She'd probably be shocked when she saw the blood all over him, and he was wrapped in a bathrobe that obviously wasn't his. But, judging from her expression, she didn't seem aware of anything but the director. If she loved him, she would forgive him.

Then I got as far away from that house as possible, went home, and scanned the news for a report about the murder of The Honorable Savannah Braddock, newest and youngest judge in an outlying county in the second circuit court. I waited all night, and it never came. It wasn't on the late night news. Had anybody discovered the body yet? Had the director instructed one of his henchman to get rid of it? Should I make the call? The thought of that poor woman decomposing in her bedroom made me sick. I wondered how long it had taken her to die. I couldn't eat. I couldn't sleep. I kept seeing her lifeless, unclothed body before my eyes. I couldn't stop seeing it.

The next morning I went in to work, and Peggy called me into her office.

"Close the door," she said. Peggy never closed her door. It wasn't a good sign. I wasn't even seated when she lit into me.

"I left you in charge of the office yesterday, and I find out you left it unattended."

"It was a family emergency."

"That's funny, because when I talked to the director this morning, he said you were helping him on a special project he couldn't discuss, but that he was very impressed with you. In fact, he's putting you up for a promotion."

That came as a complete shock.

She peered into my eyes. "You didn't know? What is this all about? Are you after my job? Or are you after him? You're just his type."

I was horrified. "No, absolutely not. I have no interest in the director or your job. The director called asking for you, and you weren't here. He needed a ride, so I offered to help."

"I get the feeling there's more to the story."

I wasn't talking. If the director had wanted Peggy to know, he'd have told her.

"May I go now? I have a press release to write."

The puzzled look on her face told me she didn't know what I was working on, which must have exacerbated her feeling that she didn't have her finger in every pie and that she was no longer in control, but she let me go anyway.

Now I was in hot water with my boss. So the director thought he could buy me off with a promotion? I shrugged. Murder and dirty politics were above my pay grade. But I wasn't complaining. I could use the money.

I walked back to my desk, where no press release waited. I could always see if Stanley needed any help. I shouldn't have worried. There was always something going on around this office. Any minute the phone would ring, signaling an inmate had escaped or killed another inmate or stabbed a correctional officer or started a riot. When I first came to work for her, Peggy, noting how naïve I was, warned me about the inmates employed around the Division office on the work release program. "They're all going to claim they're innocent. Don't believe them." The phone rang in

Peggy's office. Her door was still open. She turned white as a sheet. The news about Savannah Braddock was out.

I could hear her making frantic phone calls to her posse. "Did you hear anything?" "When did it happen?" "The director must be devastated." "Who found her body? I can't believe it."

No one wanted to know the answer to those questions more than me. But I wasn't in Peggy's inner circle. I pretended to keep myself busy rifling through a file I had hastily picked up off my desk. But images of Savannah's naked body continued to haunt me.

"Oh, my God." "Who do you think did it?" "When is the funeral?" "Have you seen the director since—" Peggy closed the door. She was going to keep the juicy details to herself.

Then I began to worry. What if the police started asking me questions? What would I say? That I had been with the director all morning? That's what he expected me to say, but I was a terrible liar. Could the police even get in the door? Who had jurisdiction? Could the director keep the police out?

"Did you hear the news?" Stanley asked, hovering over my desk.

I shook my head.

"Savannah Braddock was murdered."

I tried my best to look shocked. That was easy to do. I was still traumatized. "Do they know who killed her?"

"They think it might be someone she convicted and sent to prison. Or maybe it was a robbery. She was in the wrong place at the wrong time."

"That makes sense," I said, in a daze.

Across the hall from our office, we maintained a roomful of hanging desk files. In these files were duplicates of the inmate records in the institutions that housed them, complete with additional facts like name, race, sex, hair color, eye color, height, weight, birthdate, and all of the aliases, marks on the inmate's face, including descriptions of tattoos like crosses, lightning bolts, swastikas, skull flames, and Vikings.

We had a file on each inmate with his or her DC number, name, the date the person was received into the system, the inmate's age, offense, date sentenced, county, and the sentence imposed, and if there was one, the date of parole. We kept the files as background, and because, more likely than not, the inmates would end up back in the system for another offense. And they came in handy when law enforcement wanted to round up the usual suspects.

We undoubtedly had some recent escapees who would fit the bill in this case. I wanted to hang around and get the latest news. I also wanted to go home and think things over. I wanted to talk to my boyfriend, if he was even still my boyfriend. I grabbed my purse and gave Jean some lame excuse about an emergency.

"Another one?" she asked. Apparently, she'd heard me give Peggy my excuse about my whereabouts yesterday. Let her think what she wanted. I was getting out of there, and I didn't care what anyone thought.

As I walked out the door, I ran smack into a brick wall—an immovable pair of shoulders. I would have tripped had the director not caught me in his grasp.

"How are you holding up?"

"I heard they found her," I whispered into his chest.

"Yes. One of her coworkers went to her apartment when she didn't show up for court. You look like hell, by the way," he said.

"I didn't sleep," I replied. "Have they—" I didn't seem to be able to put a coherent sentence together with the director standing so close. I could understand why Savannah Braddock had fallen under his spell. He was both mesmerizing and terrifying at the same time.

"The police are looking for a family member of someone she convicted. Or a recent escapee. They're going over the records now."

I frowned. We both knew it wouldn't produce the real killer.

"I was nowhere near the scene. We were working together that morning. You remember. I doubt the police will even question you. Have you talked to Peggy?"

"About my promotion?"

"Well deserved."

Sure it was. After all, I'd been working there four whole weeks.

"Are you staying here?"

"Right now, *here* is the last place I want to be," I admitted. "I'm going home. I couldn't sleep last night."

He released my shoulders. It was then I could see the toll the previous day had taken on him. His eyes were bloodshot and his face bloodless. He nodded his head in understanding. "I'll be in touch."

I backed away, and he strode over to Peggy's office and knocked on the door, no doubt going in an attempt to smooth things over.

"Director, I'm so sorry." Those were the last words I heard before she admitted him into her inner sanctum and accepted a hug.

So was I. Sorry I'd ever come to work there.

Chapter Six

"I'd like to speak to Daniel Krantz, please."

The girl on the other end of the line called out, "Hey, Danny. Phone call."

Danny? I wondered what she looked like. And I wondered why there was a girl at the end of the line in his house at all. And why she sounded so at home. He never told me he had female roommates. And I wondered how many other girls there were in the house or in his life. With all the late night studying and drinking and smoking, who knew what all else was going on? By the time I heard Daniel's voice I had worked myself into a jealous frenzy.

"Who is this?"

"It's only been a month. Have you forgotten me already?"

"Merritt, is that you?"

"Yes, it's me. Who was that girl?"

He hesitated. "Oh, just a girl."

"Does she live there?" His silence spoke volumes.

"I didn't know you had a female roommate."

"I told you about her. You must have forgotten."

"I think I would have remembered that. Have you?"

"Have I what?"

"Forgotten. About me. About us."

"Of course not. I miss you."

"Do you?"

"Yes, why would you say that?"

"Because you hardly ever call me. I'm stuck in this godforsaken town all by myself, and I'm afraid I'll never get out of here. And—we need to talk."

"That sounds serious. Talk about what?"

"Everything. Us. I mean, when am I going to see you next?"

"Thanksgiving. I'll be home for Thanksgiving."

"Yes, well, Thanksgiving is four months away, and your home is Miami, but I don't live there anymore. I live in Nowheresville."

"Merritt, you were the one who wanted to take that job. I told you, you could come to Virginia."

"And do what? Sit around while you study? I got a college education, and I want a career. I can't get a job in my field there. I did try."

"What do you want me to do about it? I didn't tell you to major in PR."

"We could get engaged," I blurted out. I couldn't believe I said that, but this conversation was getting nowhere. Long-distance calls were outrageously expensive, and I was paying for this one. I needed to get right to the point.

"Engaged?" I could almost hear him choking. "I have three years of law school in front of me. That would be premature."

"Well, if you really loved me, you wouldn't want to be apart for three years."

"I don't want to be apart. I miss you. Hey, I have a great idea. Why don't you check the ride board at FSU and hitch a ride up here? We could spend the weekend together."

As tempting as that sounded, if I knew Daniel, we would spend the weekend in bed, and I would be no closer to getting a ring on my finger than I was when I got there. Sure, he missed me. He missed sleeping with me. Although he probably had plenty of girls up there who would oblige him. Who may already have obliged him.

"Well, what do you say?"

"I have to think about it."

"Don't you want to see me?"

"Of course I do. But I really need to talk to you about—"

"Krantz," yelled a guy. "You're hogging the phone. Tracy says you have a study date."

"Shit," I heard Daniel swear.

"A study date? And who is Tracy?"

"Just a girl."

"The girl who answered the phone?"

"No, another girl."

"Another roommate?" The silence was deafening.

"You're going on a date with her?"

"Merritt, it's not a real date. It's a study date. We have a midterm coming up."

"A study date?" I was furious. Most of our study dates in college had turned into make-out sessions and more. I needed to get this mess about Savannah's death off my chest, and my boyfriend was going off on a date with another woman.

I knew it was an immature thing to do, but I hung up. Right there. Just like that. The problem was I was still hung up on the bastard, and I knew I would drive right over to the FSU student union in Tallahassee and see if anyone was advertising a ride to Charlottesville,

Virginia, for the weekend. Because the sad, honest truth was I needed a weekend of mind-blowing sex, of lying against Daniel's familiar body, to be held and soothed by him, skin to skin, naked and satisfied. It was only then, in the air of intimacy, that I could confide about the murder and get it off my chest.

Chapter Seven

"Thanks for the ride," I said, stretching to get the kinks out of my back and unfolding my cramped legs. We agreed to meet at the same place on Sunday morning. I paid the driver for half the gas and walked up to the house. It was right across the street from the law school, and bigger than I had imagined.

Daniel opened the door.

"Baby," he said, pulling me into his arms and kissing me. "God, I missed you." He picked up my overnight bag and dragged me into his bedroom. He shut and locked the door and started pulling off my clothes.

"Hello, you," I said.

"Hello," he said and smiled. "First things first." He pulled off my T-shirt and my bra and filled his hands with my breasts. "I missed these," he said, kissing me. Then he pulled down my jeans and pulled off my panties and rubbed up against me. He was definitely glad to see me.

Then he pulled off his shirt, pulled down his jeans, and threw off his underwear. He jumped into his single bed and pulled me down on top of him and then reversed positions and kissed me some more. He began arousing me with his hands and his lips and his tongue, and it was like we had never been apart. I held him tight, and he entered me and I cried out.

47

"Sorry," I said, not wanting to disturb his roommates.

"Don't worry. They knew you were coming." And then we both laughed. "What I meant was—"

"I know what you meant." We were lying on our backs, shoulder to shoulder, staring up at the ceiling.

"Boy, that felt great," he said. "I don't ever want to leave this room."

"I'm starving," I argued.

"Okay, then, I'll order out."

"When am I going to meet your roommates?" And by the tone of my voice he knew I meant his female roommates.

"I don't want to share you with anybody yet."

"Are we going to spend the whole weekend in your bedroom?" Not that I was complaining.

"Would that be so bad?"

"Well, no."

"Admit, it, baby, you missed me, too. I could tell."

"All right, I missed you."

"When do you have to leave?"

"First thing Sunday morning."

"We only have one full day together."

"And two nights."

"Well, let's make the most of them. Let's take things slow," he whispered. And he started moving on me again, touching my breasts, kissing my nipples, and moving his mouth lower, rubbing me gently until I came again. I twined my legs around him, moving my body restlessly against his, taking him into my hands and stroking until he got his release. I never wanted this feeling to end. I didn't realize how much I'd needed him.

"What if I told you I didn't want to go back?" I said, biting my lip.

"I wish you could stay. Of course I do. What about your job?"

"Well, I really don't want to go back to Watertown. And there's something I need to tell you."

Daniel sat up in bed. "You're not pregnant, are you?"

"What?"

"You said there's something you need to tell me. Isn't that how the conversation usually goes?"

"I'm on the pill, silly. No, that's not it. But would it be so bad if I were?"

"What would you do?"

"Your use of *you* is not reassuring. *We'd* have to figure it out."

"I'm paying for law school. I can't afford a family right now."

"Don't worry, but that's part of what I want to talk to you about."

I sat up and covered myself with a sheet. I looked around at the mess, Daniel's dirty laundry was everywhere—on the floor, on his desk, scattered socks, wrinkled shirts, mixed with piles of paper. I hadn't even had time to take a tour, but I'd glanced at the kitchen on my way to the bedroom, and it was as untidy as Daniel's room. The place was a pit. I couldn't live here. But I couldn't live in Watertown, without Daniel, not for three more years.

"Daniel, I need to know where I stand. I mean, are we together?"

"I don't think we could get much closer." He toyed with my nipple.

"I'm not talking about sex," I protested. "I mean are we a couple? Are we going to end up together after you graduate from law school? Are we going to get married?"

"That's the plan."

"Then why can't I just stay here with you? I can get a job, any job."

"I thought you wanted to work in your profession."

"I do, but—"

"Don't you like your job?"

It's not the job I don't like. I was learning a lot, but after the murder, I didn't think I could stay on that job, working for a man who could end someone's life like that with his large, hard, cold hands and a handy deadly weapon. It obviously wasn't premeditated. It seemed, to me, to be a crime of passion. The director had come for his usual tryst with his lover and something had gone terribly wrong. Savannah demanded a commitment. She threatened to leave him for another man. The director couldn't tolerate rejection. Was that the way it had gone down? No matter what happened, I couldn't keep this secret and stay in that place. What if the director wanted to tie up loose ends? I was the only loose end that could put him at the scene of the crime. A man that powerful, with powerful friends, could make a girl like me disappear. They could blame it on an inmate, like they were for Savannah's death.

"I like my job," I began. I started to tell him about my promotion, then rethought it. How could I justify getting promoted in such a short time on the job? That would have looked suspicious. Then I knew I had to keep the secret. I didn't want to involve another person and put Daniel's life in jeopardy. "But I miss you."

He caressed me. "I miss you too, but I barely have enough money to live on here, with the tuition, and it will take me a while to pay back the loans. And I wouldn't have any time to spend with you. I'm studying all the time. I haven't even had a chance to go into town. I've never even seen downtown C'ville."

"C'ville?"

"Charlottesville."

It had only been a month, and Daniel already had inside expressions I knew nothing about. We were growing farther apart every day.

"Isn't Charlottesville adjacent to the campus?"

"The undergraduate campus, yes. And it's not called a campus. The law school is off grounds."

"Off grounds?"

"Mr. Jefferson called it grounds, not campus. The law school is in the north grounds."

"Oh, I see, *Mr. Jefferson* called it *grounds*."

"The law school was founded by Thomas Jefferson."

"I *knew* that," I reminded. Daniel could be infuriating sometimes and annoyingly smug. "But you'll get a great job after law school, and then you can pay back your loans. We can pay them back together."

"I have to get through this semester first. And then next year is a mad dash to get a second-year internship to become a summer associate."

"Evan and Kate are getting married. He's in law school, and they're going to live in married housing."

"Evan's parents are paying their way. And he goes to Florida. UVa Law is expensive. And I'm paying out-of-state tuition."

"I don't think I can wait for three years."

Daniel put his hand on my cheek. "What are you saying, Merritt?"

"I might have to move on with my life."

He dropped his hand abruptly. "Have you met someone?"

I raised my chin. "There are a lot of men in the division." *Mostly inmates on the work release program.* I hadn't seen one eligible man, except for the director, and he was married, had been having an affair, *and* he was a murderer. Besides the fact he was old enough to be my father.

"Are you breaking up with me? Is that why you came here, to do it face-to-face?"

I blew out a breath. "You don't understand."

"Make me understand, then."

"All my friends are either engaged or already married. I can't wait around forever."

"I'm not asking you to wait forever."

"Three years seems like forever."

"Baby, come here." He opened his arms, and I fell into them. Then my tears started falling.

"Don't cry. We can get engaged, if that's what you want."

"It should be what *you* want too."

"I do want that. But I can't afford a ring right now."

"I don't care about the ring." I just wanted some certainty in my life.

He squeezed me in a comforting bear hug.

"You've been traveling all day. And you said yourself you're starving. Let's get you something to eat. Then we'll go into C'ville. I actually want to see it myself. They say it's just like Gainesville. We can take a walk around, get something to eat, get the kinks out—if you have any kinks left." He laughed. "And I haven't even shown you the house. You haven't met my roommates. Tomorrow there's a toga party at one of the seniors' houses."

"I don't have a toga," I sniffled.

He unwound the sheet slowly from my naked body. "*Et voilà!* Just wrap this around yourself. Instant toga." He started chanting, "Toga. Toga. Toga."

"You might have to wash it," I said, smirking.

"There, now that almost looks like a smile. Come on, baby, let's get out of here."

At that point I would have gone anywhere with him. I knew just how the weekend would go. We'd eat, walk around, and jump right back into bed. Spend the weekend exploring each other's bodies, bodies that had been starving for each other, and storing up the satisfaction to hold us for when we were apart. I wasn't finished with him. Tomorrow night, we'd spend an hour at the toga party, and offer our excuses to leave early so we could jump back into bed and quench our thirst for each other. I wouldn't even have time to razz him about his female roommates. We would barely have time to come up for air.

I knew I would wait for him. And he knew it too. But could I trust him enough to spill my secrets? Not yet.

I clutched him when we said our goodbyes on Sunday.

"We'll see each other at Thanksgiving," he whispered, planting a soft, meaningful kiss on my lips. "Maybe I'll have a surprise for you then." Did he mean an engagement ring?

A would-be Mario Andretti screeched up the driveway in his beat-up old VW.

"Christ, Merritt. You're going home in that?" said Daniel, looking askance at the battered piece of crap pulling up in front of the house.

"My carriage awaits," I said, wiping a fresh stream of tears from my eyes.

"More like a Formula 1® racer."

He hoisted my overnight bag into the trunk. "Drive safe," he said to the driver, eyeing him suspiciously.

"Hey, I got her here, didn't I?"

"I guess you did." Then to me, "I love you, Merritt," he said, standing at the passenger door. "See you soon. Call me when you get back to Florida." He shut the door.

"I will." I wanted to tell him. I wanted desperately to unburden myself, but it looked like I was going to have to face the consequences on my own.

Mario gave me a sidelong glance as we pulled away. "So, was it worth it?"

"What?"

"Driving all this way for a booty call."

I was tempted to say, "Get your mind out of the gutter," but instead I pursed my lips into a Mona Lisa smile and said, "Definitely."

"Looks like Lover Boy got lucky."

Chapter Eight

"The director wants to see you in his office," Jean said, holding out a pink telephone message slip.

"When did he call?"

"About half an hour ago. You'd better get up there."

"Where's Peggy?"

"She's in with the deputy director."

"Did he say what he wanted?"

"No, just that he needed to see you right away."

I'd come in late because I was exhausted from the long trip from Virginia. The air conditioning was broken in the car, which had made the trip even more unbearable.

What could the director want? I wasn't in top form at the moment. I could easily fall asleep at my desk. I put my purse in my drawer, locked it, and was about to walk out of the office to take the elevator up to the third floor, where the executives held court, when Jean called out, "You were gone Friday, so I guess you haven't heard."

"Heard what?"

"They did the autopsy. Savannah Braddock was pregnant."

Suddenly, I couldn't breathe. I clutched at my chest. "Oh, my God. That's horrible." I snapped out of my lethargy in a hurry.

"I know. Peggy said the director was beside himself."

"He didn't know?"

"No one knew. When they catch the bastard who did it, they're going to charge him with a double homicide."

My knees had turned to jelly. I grasped the side of Jean's desk.

"Are you okay? You look ill."

I felt the bile rise in my throat.

"Hey, you'd better get on up there. The director doesn't like to be kept waiting."

I walked up to the director's office in a daze, unsure of what I'd find. All I could remember were the contours of Savannah's perfect body, her beautiful face, unmarred, still faint with the blush of sleep, her smooth fair skin, and the knife sticking out of her belly, her pregnant belly, the blood bright red against the satin sheets.

"Go right in, Merritt," said Belinda, the director's secretary. "He's expecting you."

I walked into the director's office.

"Close the door, Belinda. We don't want to be disturbed." Then to me he said, "Have a seat, Miss Saxe. Or may I call you Merritt? I think we know each other well enough for that." He looked at me accusingly. "You went out of town."

"I wasn't aware I needed your permission."

"It would be better if you stayed in the city, under the circumstances."

"It would be better if you didn't treat me like a common criminal."

"From now on, don't leave town without telling

me. How was your weekend?"

The smug bastard. I saw how it had all played out. Savannah had come to him to tell him about the pregnancy and threatened to go to his wife if he didn't marry her. The director couldn't live with the scandal, couldn't give up his cushy job or his high lifestyle. So he eliminated the problem—problems. I wasn't going to protect this monster.

"Did you call me up here to talk about my weekend?"

"You're upset. You've heard about, about Miss Braddock's condition, then."

I fixed my eyes on his like daggers. How appropriate.

"You still think I killed her? You think I killed my own baby? Christ, I lost them both." And then he broke down, sobbing, his head on his desk.

I had never seen a grown man cry. I was at a loss about what to do. What could I do?

"I was going to leave my wife and marry Savannah. I would have given up everything for her. But when I got there, she was…she was already gone."

He almost sounded sorry. I *almost* believed him. The director lifted his head from the desk and wiped his eyes on his shirtsleeves. "Has anybody called you?"

"Why would they? No one knows I was there. I have no connection to Miss Braddock."

"I don't expect they will. I have them convinced it was an inmate, someone who'd had a run-in with Savannah in court. They're going through the records now. There are plenty of candidates—violent men who are capable of doing what was done to Savannah, uh, Miss Braddock."

"But that's not what happened, is it?"

The director shrugged. "It's a place to start." The director had connections, in the police department, the sheriff's department, law enforcement throughout the state. I had no doubt he could engineer a cover-up. But he had me, just in case things fell apart. I was the alibi.

"The paperwork is on my desk. As soon as I sign it, your promotion will go into effect. Congratulations to our latest Information Specialist III."

I shook my head. "I don't deserve that. There's a man in my office who's been working there for years, and he's only an Information Specialist II."

"You're an enterprising and *loyal*—emphasis on the word loyal—young lady. You can have a promising career, if you want it."

"What about Peggy? She's bound to get suspicious."

"You let me handle Peggy. The funeral is this weekend. I'll have to go, but I don't know how I'll get through it."

I looked at a picture of Miss Julia on his desk.

"Your wife will be there, won't she?"

He grimaced. "Yes, but—I'd like you to be there."

I opened my mouth to speak, but nothing came out. After a few seconds, I responded, "I hardly knew Savannah Braddock. In fact, I never even met her formally. I have no business being there. People wouldn't expect me to attend her funeral."

"I would." Was that a direct order? Was I going to start paying for my promotion? Would there be a separate coffin for the baby? No, because the baby was unborn. Savannah Braddock's funeral was the last place I wanted to be.

"Will you come? It would mean a lot to me."

Was this some kind of trap? Later on, would the police examine film of who was at the funeral because, just like the killer always returned to the scene of the crime, wasn't the killer always at the funeral? Acting grief-stricken or at least like a sick voyeur, getting off on the grief of others? Soaking up their pain while reliving the pain of the victim? At least that was the way it always worked on TV.

"If you want me to go, I'll be there." After all, the man had just promoted me, and he was my boss's boss. Even if I was just his alibi, someone he wanted to keep under his thumb and keep a watchful eye on. He had me just where he wanted me.

He wiped his handkerchief across his face for a final time. "Thank you for your fine work, Miss Saxe," the director said, getting up and shaking my hand forcefully. Dismissing me.

"I'll be in touch," he said, as I walked toward the door. Did that mean he would call me, like one of the guys, and shoot the breeze, or invite me out for a beer, or coach me on what to say to the police when they ultimately set their sights on him as a suspect? How was an alibi supposed to act? What was an alibi supposed to do? As far as I knew, there was no alibi handbook.

When I got back to the office, Jean cornered me. "Well, how did it go?"

"It was all right."

"What did he want?"

"He wanted to promote me."

Jean's puzzled expression was laughable. "To what?"

"An Information Specialist III. Yes, I know I've only been here a short time. I know how it looks."

"Stanley's going to have a fit. He's been here for years, and he's still a II."

"Do you think he'll quit?"

"Probably not. Have you told Peggy?"

"She already knew."

"How did she take it?"

"She was probably not thrilled, but—"

Speak of the devil. Peggy roared out of her office, loaded for bear. A bear I imagined she had bagged on a hunting trip with the director.

"What did you talk to the director about?"

"Nothing, really," I answered. "Mainly about the promotion."

Jean went back to her typing. Peggy frowned. She couldn't figure it out. Of course she couldn't. It made no sense.

"Come into my office," she said. "I need you to write a press release."

I followed her into her office, expecting to be grilled again. She handed me a file and began telling me about Inmate 123 and how he had been placed on death row for the murder of his wife. The vultures of the press were beginning to circle.

"And you will be handling the press inquiries."

It felt like I'd swallowed dirt.

"Isn't that something Stanley would normally handle?" Peggy regularly wrestled with Stanley for any opportunity to deal with the media. Stanley was an experienced reporter who could handle the media because he had been one of them. Peggy couldn't stand anyone else getting mentioned in a newspaper. One less press clipping for her file. But she knew that was my least favorite part of the job.

Peggy and I had vastly different approaches to dealing with the media. She was eager to jump into the fray and do battle. I was content to sit on the sidelines and wait for the circus to pass me by. Peggy said talking to reporters was like having sex. "First you withhold information, then you tease and cajole, then you share and release information and leave them wanting more." They never taught that philosophy in journalism school. To me, talking to reporters was nothing like having sex.

At least that confirmed one thing. Peggy Springer had definitely had sex. I'd had my doubts about that. I didn't see how she had time to fit sex into her busy schedule.

Much as I hate talking to reporters, I almost burst with pride when I saw myself quoted in my first press interview. It was a simple thing. A simple answer. But there it was in black and white, "The Florida correctional system is overcrowded," said Merritt Saxe, spokesperson for the Florida Division of Corrections. I Xeroxed the article and sent it to my parents.

"You're the Information Specialist III. You can handle it."

Peggy knew I hated writing press releases almost as much as handling media calls. I was always afraid I'd say the wrong thing. Something that, once said, couldn't be unsaid. Give me a newsletter to write any day.

And this was a high profile case. I'd be on the phone for hours, sweating bullets and downing Tums. I wanted to be anywhere but here.

Was that a smirk on Peggy's face? She was enjoying my discomfort.

Chapter Nine

The course of the investigation changed dramatically when the police brought in Roy Starnes, the Division Comptroller, for questioning. It didn't take him long to point the detectives in his boss's direction. The detectives on the case were almost apologetic when they were admitted to the director's office to "rule him out" as a suspect. The director had arranged for me to be in the office working on our special "project" when they were led in.

"Gentleman, I'd like you to meet Merritt Saxe, our new Information Specialist III." He shot me a warning look. "She's here helping me with a special project that's going to change the direction of corrections for the next century. Merritt, meet Homer Chaffee and Plato Barnes."

Homer and Plato? Could there be two less philosophical-looking people? I had a feeling if I looked in a dictionary under "good old boys" I'd find Homer's and Plato's pictures. I was face to face with Andy of Mayberry and Barney Fife.

"Now, what can I do for you boys?"

Detective Homer Chaffee, who did all the talking and was obviously the man in charge, handed me his card, shuffled, and looked like he wanted to be anywhere but here. "Will, we're here about Savannah Braddock. Just thought we'd save you a trip down to the station. We, uh, talked to Roy Starnes."

"Good man, Roy."

"Yes, well, uh, Mr. Starnes led us to believe that you, uh, and the victim had a special relationship, if you know what I mean, and that we should probably take a closer look."

The director let loose with a belly laugh. "Me and Savannah? Christ, Homer, she was young enough to be my daughter. How long have you known me? I'm a happily married man. Don't you let Miss Julia hear you talking like that. She'd tan my hide. That woman has a memory like an elephant, and she sure can hold a grudge. *And* she's a crack shot. Which is why I would never mess around." Boy, the director could put on a good-old-boy accent like nobody's business. I tried to steady my hands while the director delivered the coup de grace. "Just what are you insinuatin'?"

"I'm not insinuating anything, Will. Of course I know you wouldn't do anything to dishonor Miss Julia. We just have to check on your whereabouts on the morning of the murder."

"Uh, let's see." The director looked through his calendar, rubbed his chin like he was contemplating, and fixed a faraway look on his face. He was good.

"Wait, now…Merritt? Wasn't that the morning we were working on that special project? I asked you to come to the ranch to deliver some papers, and that's when we started talking about it, you know, the special project. You remember that, now, don't you, darlin'?"

Darlin'? Now I was on the spot. I flushed and stammered, and gnashed my teeth. The room was spinning.

The director put his powerful arm around me and

pulled me close into a bear hug, winking at the detectives. "Now, don't be shy, honey. These nice gentlemen just need to get their answers, and then they'll be on their way. They've got important work to do. They're not interested in what we do in our private time."

Jesus. The big rat was implying that we, the director and me, were an item, to throw the detectives off his trail.

"Come on, tell the boys what they need to know. We don't want to hold them up." He squeezed me harder.

"Miss Saxe?" Detective Chaffee prompted.

"I, uh, well, I, um, h-he's r-right. We were working on a s-special project that morning." I inhaled a breath and might have fainted if the director hadn't been there to hold me up. It was true. That special project was a murder cover-up.

"Now, boys, there's no need to spread this around. I wouldn't want Miss Julia to get a whiff of gossip. Let's just keep this special project to ourselves."

"I *see*," said Detective Chaffee, and judging from the big smile that dawned on his face, he did see. The director was diddling his newest hire, and he didn't want Miss Julia to know about it. Apparently, that wasn't as farfetched as it seemed. I was his alibi. I had lied to the police. I was doomed.

"Would you sign a sworn statement to that effect?" Homer posed, deepening the hole.

"Of course we will," assured the director.

"Well, then, there's no need to trouble you two further," said Chaffee, extending a professional courtesy to his fellow law enforcement colleague. "I'm going to have some statements sent over for you to sign. No need to come down to the station." He turned to me. "Thanks for your time. Miss Saxe, if you can think of anything else you'd like to tell me, then you give me a call."

I could barely speak. I gave him my best deer-in-the-headlights stare, and nodded.

"Homer, I'm going to see that Miss Julia invites you and Trudy over to the ranch for drinks and dinner real soon, ya hear?"

"That would be great. Trudy would love that. She's dying to see how Miss Julia redecorated the place. Thank you for your time."

"Glad to be of service. Now, if there's ever anything I can do for you boys, anything you need, you be sure and let me know." And just like that they were gone. And I was officially a criminal, working in the criminal justice system.

The director shut the door and edged closer to me. His body almost touched mine. His aftershave gave off a powerful aroma of spearmint and man scent. I was overwhelmed.

"Now, that wasn't so bad, was it?"

Rounding on him, I found my voice and my moral high ground. "I lied to the police. I could go to jail."

"Don't worry your pretty little head, sugar. You aren't going anywhere as long as you stick to the truth and stick with me." Was that a threat or a proposition? If he was capable of killing the woman he supposedly loved, then he would have no trouble getting rid of me.

"The truth?" I blurted out. "That was definitely not the truth."

"In a manner of speaking, it was."

"Not in any manner. How could you let them think…?"

The director smiled. "That we were lovers?" He enjoyed toying with me. He tilted my chin up with his fingertip and tilted it left and then right, and his eyes slowly traversed my body. I flinched.

"Is that so hard to imagine?" he teased. "I can imagine it. In fact, I have imagined it. I'm imagining it right now."

Shit, what a gutter rat. I had to get out of there and go home and wash off the veneer of filth that was coating the room. Savannah's body was hardly cold, and he was looking to replace her with a new bedmate. Me.

"I have to go." I extricated myself from his grasp, ran to the door, opened it, and shot out.

His booming laugh followed me down the hall.

Chapter Ten

"I need to speak to Daniel Krantz." I tapped my foot silently on the shag carpet.

"Danny," a female voice shouted. "Phone for you."

Danny again? It took him almost a minute to pick up the telephone. What was he doing, zipping up his pants? Who was he with? Who was that sexy-sounding girl on the other end of the line?

"This is Danny."

"Daniel," I said, choking on my words and trying to hold back the tears.

"Merritt, baby, is that you? You're crying. What's wrong?"

"I need to see you."

"Honey, we talked about that. You were just here, and I'm coming home at Thanksgiving, which is right around the corner."

I sniffled. "I could catch another ride up."

"This isn't a good weekend. I have a major test in Contracts to cram for. And then I've got a paper due in Torts. And next week is my Property exam. I'll be up all night studying. I wouldn't even have time to see you."

Up all night with who?

"Then come to Watertown after your test."

"Honey, this is law school. You know I can't skip class. I can't afford the time."

"Well, if I was working up there, we could see each other anytime. We could move in together."

"Hold on, Merritt. We talked about this."

"I have something to tell you, and it can't wait."

"Then tell me over the phone."

"I can't tell you over the phone."

"Now you're scaring me."

"I want to quit my job. I want to be with you."

"You're painting a pretty picture, Merritt, but we're too young. I've got three years of law school ahead of me. I can't just quit and play house with you all day."

"Is that what you think I want to do? I'm in love with you. Doesn't that mean anything?"

"Of course it does."

I pouted, for all the good it did me over the phone. "There's something I have to ask you—a legal question."

"Sure, if I can answer it."

"Let's say a person vouches for another person about their whereabouts on the morning of a crime, and say that person signs a statement to that effect, but that person couldn't corroborate said person's whereabouts and lied to the police. Could that person be liable for filing a false statement?"

"What are you talking about? Is this some friend of yours? You'd better tell them not to sign a false statement. I don't actually know the consequences of swearing to a false statement. Maybe it depends on the crime. What are we talking about here?"

I hesitated, almost choking on the words. "Well, murder."

"Merr, is this some kind of a joke? I don't want

you associating with anybody like that. I know you work for the prison system, but I don't want you ending up there. I know you're not asking for yourself. Who is this person who violated the law?"

I sighed. Daniel didn't know me very well, or the new person I'd become.

"It's nothing. It's hypothetical, just a problem I ran across at work. Since you are in law school I figured you might know about something like that."

"I'd say steer clear of anyone who willfully lies under oath, either in a court of law or on a sworn statement."

"That's what I thought. Well, sorry to bother you, then. Good luck on your exams."

"I love you, Merritt. Good night."

"Good night." I cradled the phone gently when what I really wanted to do was slam it down, and I deliberately didn't say, "I love you" back. Daniel didn't understand anything. Couldn't he tell I was desperate and needed help, or at least sympathy? I wasn't about to blurt out my problem over the phone. All he cared about were his exams and his new life in Virginia, while I was wrestling with life and death matters in Nowheresville, Florida.

And speaking of states, limbo was not a very desirable state. I was still a stranger in town, and I had no friends to hang out with, or call, just the people at work, and those I definitely could not confide in, especially not Peggy. This lonely life had to end.

I made up my mind. I was going to give Daniel an ultimatum at Thanksgiving. Either get engaged or break up. I felt like a clam, living inside my head. I couldn't move forward. I liked the work, but somehow I had gotten entangled in a mess that I had no idea how to unravel.

On the bright side, there was the promotion, deserved or not. I sure could use the extra money, even though it was essentially hush money.

I went into the kitchen and started puttering around. I warmed up some soup. Soup always made me feel better. To tell the truth, which apparently I now had trouble doing, I didn't have much of an appetite. I turned off the burner and poured some soup into a bowl and took my bowl to the TV tray in front of the couch. Another mindless night in front of the TV. I could always read, but I wanted the voices on the TV to keep me company. This was not any way to live, I thought, as I sipped my soup.

Three hours later I woke up in a daze in front of the TV. I had slept the night away, again. This had to stop. Tomorrow morning I was going to go in to work, plant myself in front of the director's office, and demand he make it all go away. Sure, he frightened me. He was a killer, after all. And he had a whole army of people behind him. All I had was myself.

Chapter Eleven

"The director will see you now, Miss Saxe," said Belinda in her most formal and unfriendly tone. She was growing suspicious that all of a sudden an underling was in her boss's office at all hours of the day. She was the gatekeeper and resented the fact that the upstart, me, had instant access to her boss. It wasn't adding up.

"Miss Saxe, will you close the door behind you?" I tried not to act frightened. But alone with a killer was the last place I wanted to be. I shut the door slowly. Were the doors soundproof? Could his secretary hear me if I cried out? I looked around for weapons. I imagined the director carried a gun in his jacket.

"Have a seat. What can I do for you, Merritt?"

I stammered and refused to sit. "I came here to set the record straight."

"What record?"

"We lied on our statements to the police, and I'd like to correct that."

The director laughed. "You want to admit you lied under oath?" The director had the ability to fluster someone with his nerves of steel.

"I want to make it right. I don't want to be involved. I want you to get me out of this."

"Unfortunately, Miss Saxe, you're in it up to your pretty little neck."

I pursed my lips, and my hands flew to my throat. That sounded like a threat.

"At least help me get rid of the evidence."

The director straightened in his chair. "What evidence?"

"The picture of you and Savannah, the one inside the frame that you, I mean the killer, smashed to pieces on the floor of the condo."

"The one *you* picked up off the floor?"

"To protect you."

"Well, then, I suggest you continue protecting me. Think of it as part of your new job description." He paused. "And, Miss Saxe, I think you're under the false impression that *I* am the killer. I am *not* the killer. I was in love with Savannah Braddock. She was carrying my child. Had she lived, I would have married her."

I looked the director right in the eye. He almost sounded sincere, but I didn't believe him for a minute. If he was so innocent, why would he need me for an alibi?

"What did you do with the picture?" he asked.

"It's in the night table in my condo."

"Can you put it in a safe deposit box at the bank?"

"I don't have one."

"Well, then, get one."

I recalled the photo. It was so intimate it had made me blush just to look at it. Savannah was in a skimpy bikini, and the director's well-developed abs were visible above his tight swimming trunks. He had his arm around her, and she was smiling up at him. Someone must have taken it of the two of them. Someone who knew about their illicit relationship. It was obvious, the way the two were draped around each other, that they were involved, if not in love.

"I can't afford to have that found in my house." He was probably more afraid of his wife finding it than the two detectives that had stopped by earlier. "They'd never think to look in yours."

Chapter Twelve

"Merritt, I'm going out of town with the director for a corrections conference in South Carolina, won't be back until just in time for Thanksgiving. I'm leaving you in charge of the office while I'm gone. I need to go home and pack. We're leaving right after the trial."

"The trial?"

"The Savannah Braddock trial starts today. The director wants to be there when Roy Starnes takes the stand. You know, for moral support."

I panicked. I hadn't realized it was the trial date already.

"Are you going to the trial?"

"No time. I have a million things to take care of."

"You're leaving me in charge?"

"Yes, you're the most senior in my absence. I hope there are no crises while I'm gone, but I'm sure you can handle it. See you next week."

I almost laughed. Not a day went by at this place that we didn't have a crisis.

"What if we get any media calls? Will Stanley be here?"

"Yes, but you outrank Stanley."

My stomach turned. Maybe if I locked myself in Peggy's office and didn't answer the phone, nothing would happen. Not a fire, a murder, a kidnapping, or any number of things that could and probably would happen in my boss's absence.

Peggy was enjoying herself. Stanley was smirking. Oh, happy day.

Peggy gathered her briefcase and some papers and sailed out the door. If there was one thing she liked better than collecting her press clippings, it was alone time with the director.

I inhaled a breath.

I looked at Stanley. "Stanley, I expect you to handle any media calls that come in."

"Not a chance. You're the Information Specialist III. I'm only a II. That's above my pay grade."

"Don't be a jerk," I pleaded.

"You're on your own, Merritt."

He got that right.

"I'm in charge in Peggy's absence. So you'll deal with any media calls that come in."

Peggy knew how much I hated dealing with the media. Anyway, if Roy Starnes was scheduled to take the stand. I needed to be in that courtroom. I made a flimsy excuse to Stanley and bolted out of the office.

When Roy was sworn in, my stomach clenched. The prosecutor asked a few slow-pitch questions, establishing Roy's identity and his relationship with the victim. Then he went in for the kill. Roy was their prime suspect, and they weren't going to go easy on him.

"Mr. Starnes, did you visit Savannah Braddock on the night of the murder?"

"Yes."

The courtroom exploded.

"Was it by invitation?"

"No."

"Then why did you show up at the lady's door unannounced?"

"She forgot her scarf at the ranch at the director's Fourth of July barbecue. I thought she might need it."

"You thought she might need her *scarf* in the middle of the night?"

"Well, I didn't think. I just acted."

"You wanted another chance to see Miss Braddock, isn't that right?"

"I suppose so."

"And when you surprised her at her apartment, what was she wearing?"

Roy's pale face turned a deep shade of red. "Her n-nightgown."

"Her sheer, white nightgown? The one she was wearing the night she was murdered?"

"Y-Yes."

"Speak up, Mr. Starnes."

"Yes."

"Had you ever seen Miss Braddock in her nightgown before?"

"No, of course not."

"I can only imagine what was going through your mind."

"Objection!"

"Were you in love with Savannah Braddock? Now remember, you're under oath."

"Y-Yes," Roy admitted without hesitation.

"And did she return your feelings?"

"N-No."

"And why was that?"

"She was in love with someone else."

"And is that someone else in this courtroom?"

Roy pointed to the director.

"Let the record show the witness has identified Willard Ware Baintree, Director of the Florida Division of Corrections."

"How do you know that?"

"It was c-common knowledge."

"If it was common knowledge, then why can't we get one person in the division to testify to that fact?"

"I d-don't know." Sweat was pouring off Roy's face. He patted his forehead with a handkerchief.

"Didn't you, in fact, come to the home of Miss Braddock to profess your love, and when she told you she was pregnant with another man's child, you offered to marry her?"

"I offered to give her my name. It made me sick to think that someone had violated her and deserted her that way. That a Christian man, a married man, had done this to her."

"A man you had worked with for fifteen years? A man you looked up to and respected?"

"Y-Yes."

"And when you saw Miss Braddock in her *negligee,* and accused the director of violating her, what did she say?"

She laughed and said, "I'm in love with the director."

"And how did that make you feel when she laughed at you and rejected your very chivalrous offer?"

"I wanted to get away from her. I needed to get out of there."

"Didn't you, in fact, want to lash out at her? Didn't you pick up the first weapon you saw, which was the kitchen knife, and stab her and her unborn child to death? No one could blame you. It was clearly a crime of passion."

Roy's body shook. "No, I did not and would never do that."

"What *did* you do?"

"I left."

"Weren't you, in fact, so enraged that you wanted to kill her because you knew you would never have her and you didn't want anyone else to have her?"

Roy glared at the director like he wanted to jump out of the witness stand and choke him.

Roy's tone was measured. "I'm not a violent man."

"Mr. Starnes, Roy, love does mysterious things to people."

"That's not the way it happened."

"Then tell the court exactly how it happened."

"I walked away. I just walked away."

"You want us to believe that you just walked away? That you didn't seek revenge?"

"That's right."

"And when did you find out that Miss Braddock had been murdered?"

"The next morning when I came to work. Everybody was talking about it."

"And how did you feel?"

"Sick to my stomach. And guilty."

The courtroom erupted again.

"Order in the court," yelled the judge, banging his gavel.

"Guilty?" the prosecutor prompted. "Of her murder?"

"Guilty that I didn't stay with her and spend the

night, that I didn't protect her. If I had stayed, this never would have happened."

"No further questions for this witness."

The director and Miss Julia were sitting in the front row, holding hands, presenting a solid front for the world. I glared at the back of the director's neck, for all the good that did. He was going to let an innocent man go to prison, maybe to his death, and say nothing. I imagined Roy Starnes sitting in Old Sparky, his hands strapped down, waiting for his execution. And he expected me to say nothing. I wanted to raise my hand, to shout out, "He didn't do it. The director is the guilty one!"

But of course nothing is exactly what I did.

"This court will recess for lunch, and we'll resume back here at two o'clock."

I was going to be sick.

I made my way out of the courtroom and felt a firm hand on my shoulder.

"Miss Saxe. Is everything all right?" The skin around the director's eyes was creased, and he looked concerned, probably about his own hide, not about me.

"No, everything is not all right," I whispered.

"Miss Saxe," he said, exasperated. "Merritt. What is it going to take to convince you?"

"Willard." Miss Julia came up behind us. "We need to leave now if we're going to have lunch and be back by two. And you need to pack for your trip."

The director winced and removed his hand from my shoulder. "I'll be right along, dear."

Miss Julia glared at me. I rolled my eyes. The director, the God of the prison system, the fierce warrior, everyone's hero, was seriously henpecked. No wonder he took up with another woman. A woman a good deal more pliant than Miss Julia.

"We'll talk later," he promised.

I shrugged. No doubt we would. I was getting sick of all this intrigue, with the intimate meetings filled with lies and game playing. I just wanted out, and I was trapped for all intents and purposes.

I had told the director I wasn't going to testify to anything in court. It looked like I wasn't going to be needed anyway. No one was even looking in the director's direction. The good-old-boy network was in fine form, prosecuting the innocent and protecting the guilty. The whole thing made me sick.

I drove over to a local sandwich shop near the courthouse and ordered a pastrami on rye to go. Of course the proprietors had no idea what real pastrami tasted like. Theirs was lean and tasteless, not a bit of fat or flavor. And they typically served it cold, on white bread. With mayonnaise. Yecch. What I wouldn't give for a juicy hot pastrami on rye at Wolfie's on Miami Beach. Thanksgiving was a week away, but it couldn't come soon enough.

After the recess, the defense presented evidence of several ex-cons who might have had a motive for harming Miss Braddock. Files that came directly from the file room across from my office, files I myself had researched. But no matter how many red herrings were presented, things were looking bad for the prime suspect, Roy Starnes. The police needed a villain, and the lovesick, timid Roy Starnes fit the bill very nicely, thank you very much. No matter that Roy Starnes couldn't hurt a fly. And that I knew who had really committed the crime. No one was going to let the truth get in the way of the pursuit of justice. Roy Starnes was going down the river on his way to a date with Old Sparky. And I was the only one who could stop this runaway train.

Sitting in my car, waiting for court to restart, I wiped the excess mustard off the bread with several napkins. I could hardly eat a bite, I was so distraught. And the pastrami was so bad. God forbid someone in this town could learn how to make a decent bagel. I went back to the courthouse and dumped my inedible sandwich into the nearest trash bin.

The judge was addressing the jury, and finally I heard the words I'd been waiting for: "This courtroom is recessed until the Monday after the Thanksgiving holiday."

I ran out of there before the director could get to me and headed for the office.

My bags were already packed for Thanksgiving, I was so anxious to leave, but Peggy had left me in charge, and I was going to do my best to make her proud, over the next couple of days. So I did my time at Peggy's desk and, miracle of miracles, nothing bad happened. Not even a mini-crisis, the kind that set my heart racing and got Peggy's juices flowing. I was content with the status quo.

Peggy returned Wednesday afternoon, energized no doubt by the one-on-one time she'd spent with the director, and I raced to my car to get a jump on the holiday traffic. By tomorrow, the turnpike would be clogged with travelers. I had a solid six-hour drive, but anything was better than being stuck in Watertown over the Thanksgiving holiday. My mother was a great cook, and after our family dinner, Daniel was picking me up, and we were going to park at the Miami airport along with all the other couples who had nowhere more private to go to get their release in the darkness. And after that, I was going to propose to Daniel, or at least get him to propose to me, or issue the promise of a proposal.

Chapter Thirteen

It was great to be home and surrounded by family and some of the best food I'd tasted since I left Miami. The turkey and stuffing were delicious, accompanied by biscuits, mashed potatoes, sweet potatoes, green beans, and followed of course by the tasty assortment of pies—coconut cream, pumpkin, and key lime. I was stuffed and sleepy but excited about seeing Daniel. When he arrived at my house, he spent some time talking to my parents and, impatient to be alone, we finally left together. He drove to the empty lot across from the Miami airport and parked. But we didn't spend any time watching the airport lights or the planes taking off or landing.

"I missed you, Merritt," Daniel said. He had undressed me in record time, and we had just made love in the back seat. Our slick bodies were tangled together. "And I missed this."

"I missed you, too," I said, breathless. "I wish we could be together like this all the time."

"We will be."

"I can't wait two and a half more years," I complained, wasting a pout that couldn't be seen in the dark.

"Merritt," he said, fondling me. I thought I was in a good negotiating position, as we were both still naked and sated.

"I know what you're going to say. You have to finish law school, blah, blah, blah. But how do I know you won't find another girl while I'm waiting for three years? How do I know you haven't already found someone else?"

I folded my arms under my breasts.

Daniel silenced me with a kiss. "You know you're the one, the only one."

Another wasted pout. "I need more."

I could feel his smile on my lips, and then his lips licked my nipple and locked onto my breast. "You're not satisfied?" he mumbled. "Let me see what we can do about that." His hand went lower, and I moaned. Then he moved my hand down to caress him, and by the way he responded, he made it clear he and his buddy were up for another round.

"Exactly what kind of promise do you want, baby?" he said.

"Daniel, that's not what I mean, and you know it. I need a commitment. I can't hold out for three years without a promise of something."

He stopped in mid-motion, and then I felt his frown. He pulled us both up to a sitting position.

"Do you want a ring?"

"Only if you want to give me one."

"There's something else I want to give you right now, if you'd just relax."

Sure, I was as horny as the next person, and I definitely wanted what Daniel had to give me. But I wanted more.

"I thought that's what you wanted too."

"Merritt, honey, I want the whole works with you. But right now I have to concentrate on finishing law school and getting a job. I'm focusing on our future."

"I feel like you're moving on in your life and leaving me behind, out in the cold."

He put his arms around me. "Baby, let me warm you up." He kissed my lips and tried to divert my attention by kissing me all over my body. "I think I know what you need, Merritt."

"No," I said, pushing him away. "I don't think you do. I'm tired of waiting. I want to start our life together now, and if that's not what you want too, then take me home."

"Merritt, you don't mean that."

"Yes, I do."

Daniel sighed in frustration. "Okay."

We each began dressing. I climbed into the front seat, and Daniel followed, into the driver's seat.

"Who have you been talking to?"

"I haven't been talking to anyone."

"Is it because Evan and Kate are getting married? And Deb and Donny just got engaged?"

"No," I insisted. "But those are two very good reasons. If you really loved me, you would marry me, or at least we could become engaged. I don't want to go back to Watertown." I felt like a broken record. How many times did I have to say the same thing?

"Is there something wrong at work?"

I bit my lip. Here was the perfect opportunity to tell him about my boss and the cover-up. But I was too mad to confide in him.

"I want to come up to Charlottesville. I can find a job there."

Daniel started the car.

"You have a great job in your field. You're not

going to find another public relations job in Virginia, in this economy."

"I don't care about the job. I care about you. And obviously you don't care about me."

"Merritt, we're wasting time. We only have tonight to be together alone like this. I have to spend the rest of my vacation with my family."

"All you care about is sex. That's not what I mean."

"Okay, obviously something is wrong and I don't know what it is. We had a plan to wait until I finished law school and then we'd get married."

"Well, plans change."

"Merritt. I love you, but I can't afford a wife, not now."

"You could if you wanted to. We could find a way."

Daniel drove out of the parking lot, past all the other cars with all the other lovers making love, sharing plans, or arguing. Once he was back in heavy Miami traffic, he focused on the road.

When we pulled up to my house, he stopped the car and turned to kiss me goodnight.

I pushed him away.

"Merritt, is this how you want to leave things?"

"No, but apparently you do."

"I'll call you tomorrow."

"Don't call me," I snapped, opening the car door.

"Merritt!" he shouted, but I turned my back on him and walked to the front door. I fumbled for my keys and finally let myself in without a backward glance. It was very dramatic, but I was only hurting myself. I would cry later, but not in front of Daniel. This night did not go as planned. I had been so certain it would end with a proposal. But instead, it just ended everything. Daniel did call repeatedly throughout the weekend, but I didn't take the calls, and I didn't see him before he flew back to Virginia and I drove back to Watertown.

I guess we were officially broken up. Now he had the freedom to flirt, to find someone else. I was sick about the whole thing, even though I knew I had only myself to blame.

Chapter Fourteen

I was back in the courtroom. I had to take another day off, since there was no official reason for me to be there. Peggy certainly didn't understand why I needed to go to court, but she suspected it had something to do with the director, something she wasn't privy to. It had her puzzled, but she didn't refuse my request.

Things were looking bad for Roy Starnes. The prosecution was constructing a timeline. Savannah Braddock had attended the director's barbecue the night before she was murdered. Sometime that evening or in the early morning hours she was visited by Roy Starnes, and then she was found dead the next morning.

What they left out was the fact that she, Merritt Saxe, had received a call from the director to pick him up at the victim's condo that morning, and that he had appeared at the door in a bloodstained shirt. And that they hadn't called the police. How long after Roy's visit had the director arrived? Did he in fact discover her body, or did he murder her? I knew the answer to that question, but it was as if I were stuck in stone. I couldn't move; I couldn't talk. I was going to let poor innocent Roy Starnes go to jail, or worse, for a crime he didn't commit. If the director had truly just discovered the body, then why didn't he call the police?

I also knew the answer to that question. Because the police would have asked what he was doing at

Savannah's condo in the morning, visiting the victim in her nightgown. If they had proof of the personal relationship between the director and the victim, chances were Roy Starnes would be a free man. I was the only one who had that proof.

The defense was parading all kinds of character witnesses. The highlight was when Willard Ware Baintree took the stand and, under oath, swore to the jury that the Roy Starnes he knew, who had worked for him for fifteen years, was incapable of hurting anyone. It was still his contention that a relative of one of the men Miss Braddock had sent to prison was the killer.

The director had the jury eating out of his hands. If they had cast the part of Willard Ware Baintree in a movie, the director could have played himself. She could almost see the women on the jury swooning, glued to his every word. Willard Ware Baintree was a superstar in Watertown.

In the end, Roy Starnes was found not guilty, and the case remained unsolved.

I looked at the director, and he looked relieved that an innocent man, a man on his staff, had been spared. He smiled.

So here I was, back at work, without a boyfriend, in a town I hated, working for a boss I didn't especially like, with the head of the division a person I didn't trust. But I planned to put one foot in front of another and keep going. I didn't have a choice. If I wanted a change, if I didn't want to end up a spinster, I needed a plan. I was going to have to start paying attention to other men.

Back then, they didn't have match.com or J-Date, and I didn't want to get picked up at a bar or even a bowling alley, which Watertown actually had. But Watertown Lanes offered slim pickings. So I had a good job and no love life. Could I live with that?

When I got back to my desk, I looked around the office and recalled the parade of men that used Peggy's office as a revolving door for a cup of coffee, a smile, and some juicy gossip. But as good looking, macho, and rugged as some of them were, I didn't see any romantic prospects.

If I stayed in Watertown, I would end up like Peggy. Unless I wanted to marry a prison superintendant or a correctional officer or an inmate on the work release program. Or a sheriff. I sighed. Not that there was anything wrong with those men. Sexy as some of them were, we had nothing in common.

Just then, the director came down from the third floor and into Peggy's office. On his way in, he nodded to me. Doodling on my notepad, I noticed his muscles bulging out of his white dress shirt and the planes and angles of his chiseled face. He was in great shape for a man his age. I could see why all the women at the division were crazy about him. I looked through the glass into Peggy's office and focused on the director, who was gesturing with his hands. Hands I imagined caressing my body, his lips on mine. Great. Now I was fantasizing about a killer.

"Merritt, I've been calling you." Jean's insistent voice penetrated my daydreams. "Where were you just now?"

"Right here at my desk," I replied, blushing, looking away from the window.

For heaven's sake, the director was married. To a stone-cold cookie, according to Peggy, but nevertheless, he was unavailable. Not to mention he had been cheating on his wife with a woman he ended up killing. Was that the kind of man I wanted in my life or in my bed? Or did I just need a man, and any man would do? Was I that horny? Or that lonely? The answer was a resounding *Yes!*

"Merritt," Jean admonished.

"I'm listening."

"Peggy wants you to look over this press release and arrange a press conference. She has an important announcement."

"Where's Stanley?"

"Peggy specifically requested that you do it."

"Of course she did," I whispered under my breath. *Because she knows there's nothing I hate more than dealing with the media.*

I glanced at the news release. Wow, this was big. The division was overcrowded. They were opening up a tent city to hold the overflow. That had never been done before.

"Peggy and the director are in there talking about the idea right now."

I handed back the release to Jean. "It looks good to me. I'll start contacting the reporters."

What I really wanted to do was leave Watertown. But if I left the job before a year was up, I would look flighty. I'd have to stick it out for at least a year to get this job on my resume. But every time I thought about Savannah Braddock in that bloodstained nightgown, I was more convinced than ever that I couldn't remain here. I would call the university alumni job bank and see what positions were open in my field.

I made the call the next morning. They were

advertising an opening with the Water and Sewer Division in their PR office in West Palm Beach—which, thanks to my sudden promotion, didn't pay as much as I was getting now—and an entry level job with a prestigious public relations firm in Miami. That sounded promising, but an applicant had to speak Spanish to be qualified for that position. I wasn't fluent, and I didn't relish the only other alternaive—coming home with my tail between my legs. A quitter. A failure. Looked like I was stuck in Watertown until something better came along.

I was deep in thought when the director sauntered up to my desk.

"Are you enjoying the work here, Miss Saxe?"

I looked up at him, brooding. "Yes, thank you."

"I hear good things about you from your boss."

I frowned. "From Peggy?"

"Yes, I told her to look out for you."

I expelled a breath. I was sure if it weren't for the director, Peggy would have fired me weeks before. "Thank you."

"Now, you call me if you need anything."

"I'll be sure and do that," I said, deadpan.

The director wasn't even out the door when Peggy came rushing over.

"What is it between you and the director? Why is he so concerned about you?"

"I have no idea."

"How are you coming on that tent city press conference? The director is going to be there, so it has to run smoothly."

"Don't worry. I'll handle it." I was thinking how much I was going to screw things up and make everybody look bad.

When I got home, I was exhausted. I was tired of being alone, eating alone and having no one outside of work to talk to. So Daniel caught me at a vulnerable moment when I answered the phone. I hadn't spoken to him since our breakup over Thanksgiving.

"Merritt?"

"Yes."

"It's Daniel."

"I know."

"So I was wondering whether you're coming home over winter break."

"I'm not in college anymore. I have a regular job. We don't get off for winter break."

"I just meant are you planning to come home for the holidays?"

"I guess I could."

"I'd like to see you. I'll be home on the sixteenth and don't have to be back in Virginia till after the first of the year."

"I might be able to get away for a few days around Christmas. Maybe you could drive back to Watertown with me."

There was a pause in the conversation. Right. Why would anyone want to come to Watertown?

"I'll talk to my parents about it. They'll want to spend as much time as they can with me while I'm home."

And if I were still your girlfriend, I might want the same consideration.

"So you'll see me?"

"Why not?"

"You don't sound very excited."

I didn't answer. "So how's law school?"

"It's hard. I spend every minute studying."

I'll just bet you do. I wonder how many of your study partners are women? Not to mention some of your roommates are women. I'm sure not every *minute is spent studying. Considering I don't trust you as far as I can throw you, I highly doubt you're living the life of a celibate. While, I, on the other hand, am horny as hell.*

"Merritt?"

"I'm still here."

"I miss you. I miss us."

I didn't know what to say to that, so I said nothing. Did I miss him? Sure, but I didn't hear a proposal, and until I did, I wasn't going to take him back.

"So I guess I'll see you soon."

"I guess you will."

After we hung up, I felt an overwhelming feeling of emptiness. I wished I had said more, but if he wasn't ready to make a commitment, then I wasn't going to just hang around for three years until he got in the mood to marry me.

I warmed up some soup and ate a bowl of it with crackers. My life was pathetic, but I was trapped here until something better came along or until I was ready to make a move.

When I went in to work in the morning, there was an invitation on my desk from the director. He was hosting a holiday party at the ranch, and I was invited. I looked at everyone's desk, and it looked like I wasn't the only person who received one. I was invited to bring a guest. That would be great if I had a significant other, or even anyone I knew. I'd been in Watertown for almost half a year, and I had no one to take to a holiday party. How pathetic was that? I looked at the date. I could attend the party and still make it home for a few days to see my family and Daniel. I thought it would be good for my career if I attended, and I assumed the director would not have invited me if he didn't want me there. Or maybe it was a command performance. He probably expected me to be there. So now all I needed was a date.

I spent the rest of the day calling reporters and inviting them to the press conference that would announce the opening of Tent City. Tents had already gone up, and inmates had been transferred there. Reporters were going to be given a tour by the director, who would talk about Tent City as a solution to alleviate overcrowding in the prison system. Media outlets from all over the world were sending reporters. It was an innovative idea, and it was getting a lot of attention. Stanley, Jean, and I were busy assembling press kits. Jean ordered box lunches from a nearby restaurant and had arranged for a mike and chairs to be set up and press passes to be prepared. We were already getting media inquiries. I was quoted in several newspapers. Peggy got most of the coverage, but it was exciting to see my name in print.

I took my invitation into Peggy's office. "Are you going to the director's holiday party?"

Was she going? Of course she was. She wouldn't miss another opportunity to see the director.

"Do you have a date?" I asked.

"Yes, I'm going with the superintendant of the Community Correctional Institution in Jacksonville," she said, adding, "but just as friends."

"Do you have to bring a date?"

"Don't you have one?" she asked. "What about your boyfriend?"

"He's in law school in Virginia. And anyway, he's not my boyfriend anymore. We broke up."

Peggy almost looked sorry.

"I don't really know anyone to ask," I said.

"Hey, let me call Four and see if he has anyone he can fix you up with."

"Who's Four?"

"That's the superintendent's name."

I felt like a charity case, but I agreed. "What kind of name is Four?"

"His full name is Vance Goodspeed the Fourth, but everyone calls him Four. Just hang tight. I'll let you know what he says."

I was stuffing the last press kit and placing it in the box when Peggy came up to my desk.

"Great news. The superintendant's brother lives in Watertown. He's a lawyer with the State Department of Transportation. He's about thirty."

"What does he look like?"

"How would I know? But what have you got to lose?"

"You're right. Nothing. Thanks."

"We'll all go together. We'll pick you up at six o'clock."

"What's his brother's name?"

"Israel. Israel Goodspeed."

"You sure he's not a preacher or a race car driver?"

"No, Four said he was a lawyer."

I pursed my lips and imagined what the man must look like.

"Maybe I'd better skip this one."

"You can't. It's already arranged. Anyway, aren't you curious about what the director's house looks like?"

"I've been there."

"But that was the barbecue. She's redecorated again. I'm dying to see what she did. She has all the money in the world, which is why the director married her and why he stays with her."

"How do you know that?"

"Everyone knows that."

"What are you wearing?" I asked.

"A black lace dress. What about you?"

"I'll have to go shopping. Will it be fancy?"

"Yes, Miss Julia is having it catered."

I didn't have the money to buy a new cocktail dress, but then, Watertown didn't have any dress shops. I'd have to drive to Tallahassee.

Chapter Fifteen

I don't know what I was expecting when Israel Goodspeed walked up to my door, but it wasn't this. Tall and broad-shouldered and gorgeous, he filled out his suit in the most interesting way. Comfortable in his clothes, he wore black dress cowboy boots with just the right fashion flair that looked fabulous with his outfit, a stylish white Stetson, and an attitude that said, "You got a problem with it?"

I was looking at him, looking *up* at him. In fact, I couldn't take my eyes off him. Was this the feeling people referred to as "gobsmacked"?

"Merritt Saxe?" he asked politely, taking my hand.

I thought I might melt. "That's me."

"Wow!" He smiled appreciatively, which made me blush. "My brother said you were a looker, but I had no idea you'd be this beautiful. Lucky for me."

I looked down shyly. "Thank you."

"I'm Israel Goodspeed. It's a pleasure to meet you. Are you ready to go?"

"Yes," I answered. I was ready for anything this man had to offer. He placed his hand on my back and guided me firmly but gently to the car. I shivered at his touch, even though it was a balmy evening. And he opened the door for me. Points for him for being so polite and well-mannered.

I said hello to Peggy, flashing my thanks in a

glance, then turned to her date. "Superintendant Goodspeed, it's nice to see you again."

"You can call me Four if I can call you Merritt."

"Of course," I said.

"You look mighty pretty in that dress, ma'am," Israel commented.

I bristled. "Are you seriously calling me 'ma'am'? That makes me sound like an old woman."

"It's just a Southern sign of respect," Four explained.

"And where did you get that thick Southern accent?" I asked Israel.

"What accent?" Israel wondered.

"Oh, come on. You have a definite Southern drawl."

"That's how we talk in Jacksonville. You don't have an accent at all," he noted.

"That's because I'm from Miami. That's not really considered part of the Deep South."

I turned to Israel. "So Peggy tells me you're a lawyer."

"That's right."

"My brother's being modest. He's not just a lawyer," said Four. "He's the head of his department, the youngest person to lead the department in its history. He got the brains in the family."

And the looks, too, I thought. Not that there was anything wrong with the way Four looked. But Israel had a movie-star presence. I had a feeling sex with Israel Goodspeed would be a trip to heaven. Compared to Daniel, who was just a boy, Israel was a man.

We continued to converse until, too soon, Four pulled up to the ranch.

"How about this house!" Four exclaimed.

"Wow," I said. "Valet parking. Fancy."

Israel came around to my door and offered me a hand out, while the valet got in the front seat to park the superintendant's car.

Israel kept my hand in his and led me into the house. He removed his hat, and a man took it to a makeshift cloakroom.

"I've been dying to get a look inside," Israel confided. "My brother has been bragging on the director's house."

I looked around the living room. The house certainly lived up to its reputation, even though I'd seen it once before. Since then, Miss Julia had totally redecorated. It was nothing I expected to find in a backwater place like Watertown. "That's a Chagall," I exclaimed, pointing to one of the valuable paintings on the wall. I loved the vintage design of the printed linen fabrics on the English country furniture, and the damask designer wallpaper was a perfect backdrop to provide richness and warmth in the room. "These are antiques," I said.

"How do you know so much about furniture?"

"My mother is an interior designer, for one thing, and at the Fourth of July party here, Mrs. Baintree took some of us on a personal tour of her house. She's completely redecorated and added a lot of new pieces since then, though."

A bar was set up in the corner. "Can I get you a drink?" Israel was a good escort.

"Yes, thanks, white wine would be great."

"I'll be right back. Don't go anywhere." He pressed my hand. Touchy-feely was okay with me.

"I won't."

The director came up to me. "Miss Saxe."

"Director." I nodded.

"Is that the boyfriend?"

"Nope. That's Superintendant Goodspeed's brother. There is no boyfriend anymore."

"Interesting. We'll talk later," he said, when he saw Miss Julia motioning for him across the room.

Israel returned. "That was the director, wasn't it?" Israel asked, handing me a drink.

"Yes."

"And that's the infamous Miss Julia over there?"

"It is."

"He has quite a reputation."

"In Corrections?"

"No, actually I meant with women. Four says he's a horndog, that he'll chase anything in a skirt."

"I doubt if Miss Julia would stand for that."

"What do you mean?"

"She's shooting daggers at me, and all he did was say hello."

"That she is. Let's go into the next room," he whispered. He directed her to what turned out to be a very well-stocked library. "Too many people around with big ears. You haven't heard the stories?"

"About Miss Julia?"

"About the director."

I put on my "confused" face.

"Specifically about the director and Savannah Braddock. That wasn't exactly a well-kept secret. Everyone's speculating she was carrying the director's baby."

I tried to look shocked, while I focused on the

literary wonderland around me.

I took in the many plaques and trophies placed around the room.

"Look at the names on these plaques," Israel noted. "These are all Miss Julia's. Mostly awards for marksmanship. I wouldn't want to cross her."

"I thought the director was a champion marksman."

"Everything he has or does or is came from Miss Julia. Four says she's one of the wealthiest, most powerful women in the state. There's nothing that woman does without a reason, and there's not much she wants that she can't get. She's the woman behind the man."

"Do you think she knows what goes on behind her back?"

"She's too sharp not to."

"How far do you think she'd go to stop him? I mean, what could she do if he fell in love with someone else?"

"I wouldn't want to find out."

"Peggy says the reason he stays married to her is for her money."

"And her power. He owes her everything. Even if he wanted to leave, she'd never let him."

Israel picked up a silver trophy. "She lets him play, but he'd better not stray, not permanently, at least."

I shuddered. I was already afraid of the director. I didn't know much about his wife, but I was learning.

We moved out of the library and into the den, where a roaring fireplace was going, and we sat next to each other on the couch.

"So Four says Peggy tells him you just broke up

with your boyfriend. What happened, if you don't mind me asking?"

"We dated all through college, and then he went away to law school. He has three more years, and I don't want to wait that long to be together. He wouldn't make a commitment."

He put his arm around my shoulder. "I never would have let you go."

"Have you ever been in a relationship where you—I mean, have you ever wanted to get married?"

"I've never found the right girl," he said, looking me straight in the eyes. "But when I do, I wouldn't hesitate to make a commitment."

The director came up behind us. "How are we doing here, folks?" Israel turned and shook the director's hand. "I'm Vance Goodspeed's brother Israel."

"Oh, you're Four's brother. Nice to meet you. Are you takin' good care of my girl?"

"*Your* girl?"

"Our Merritt. She's quite a woman. I hope you know what you have here."

"I do indeed, sir."

They were talking about me like I was a prize mare in my yearling spring, waiting to be mounted and bred by a famous stallion. Did they want to see me bare my teeth? Maybe my body? Although I was baring pretty much of it in my new cocktail dress. I resented the innuendos, and the director's territorial attitude, like he owned me.

"Miss Saxe. I see you're tied up at the moment. Let's talk Monday morning in my office, nine a.m., about our *special project*." The director walked away but not before he shot me a warning glance. Several more times, he peeked into the room where we were sitting and caught my eye in what seemed like a suggestive way. Was he keeping tabs on me as an alibi, or was there something more to the director's interest in me? Was he jealous of Israel's attentions toward me, or afraid of what I'd reveal?

The director popped his head in again, and this time he got an eyeful. Israel had just leaned into me and planted a possessive kiss on my lips. Caught off guard, I returned his affection.

"Is he gone?" Israel whispered.

"Who?"

"The director."

I looked up and caught the director's scowl on his way out of the room. "Yes."

"What was that all about? If I'm not mistaken, that man is acting improperly possessive toward you. I hope he got an eyeful. He's your boss, isn't he?"

"My boss's boss."

"If you have any problems with him, I want you to let me know."

"I will."

"Four thinks that man walks on water, and that he would walk through fire for him. Seems like a jerk to me. I don't like the way he looks at you."

"It's nothing," I said, dismissing the director's obvious interest in me. But it wasn't anything I hadn't thought myself. The director was getting a little too cozy for my taste.

"Was that kiss just for the director's benefit?"

He turned to me and took my chin in his hand. "What do you think?"

I was shaking. I'd never been kissed quite like that before. I was still reeling from the experience. "I don't know what to think."

"Just for the record, I've been dying to do that ever since I laid eyes on you."

"Oh." I took a minute to simmer down and change the subject. "It seems like you're pretty close with your brother."

"Four was my guardian angel growing up. No one messed with me when Four was around. If anyone ever teased me, or looked at me funny, Four would make sure they regretted it. My big brother would do anything for me and I for him."

"I'm an only child, so I never had anyone to look out for me."

He looked at me intently. "Well, now, that's all about to change."

Israel Goodspeed was making assumptions, but somehow I didn't mind.

"You don't look like you need protecting," I said.

"Well, you know how kids can be. Until I grew into my body and learned to defend myself, I got teased a lot."

From where I sat, Israel Goodspeed had certainly grown into his body.

"I can't imagine anyone picking on you."

"I wasn't always this good-looking," he said, smiling.

"Oh, really?"

"Yeah. I was a pretty scrawny kid."

"I find that hard to believe."

"What about you?"

"Me? Believe it or not, I had thick glasses and

braces on my teeth until I was in eighth grade. I was pretty much a social mess in most respects. I was skinny and shy."

"Well, now, it looks like you've grown into *your* body quite nicely, Miss Saxe," Israel said, his frank appraisal causing me to blush again. "Still shy, though," he said, smiling and crushing me against his shoulder. His man scent—or his cologne, or whatever he was wearing—was invading my senses. The pheromones were definitely flying. I was drawn to him by some invisible force.

We didn't mingle much with the crowd, just spent time sitting in front of the fire trading stories and getting to know each other. Israel brought me some hors d'oeuvres and kept the drinks coming. I had never enjoyed myself more. I didn't want the evening to end, but before I knew it, Four appeared and told us it was time to go.

"I hate to break you two lovebirds up, but I've got an early morning and a long drive back to Jacksonville."

Reluctantly, Israel helped me up off the couch, held my hand, retrieved his hat, and led me out to the car.

"Merritt, I had a great time tonight." He looked like he wanted to say more but couldn't in front of Four and Peggy.

"So did I." We held hands on the car ride home, and his body warmth wrapped me in a tight cocoon. We dropped Peggy off first.

When the car pulled up to my apartment, Israel walked me to the door.

"I had a wonderful time. I can't remember a time I

enjoyed myself more," I said and meant it.

"Can I call you? I'd like to see you again."

"I'd like that."

Mr. Yummy leaned in until his mouth was dangerously close to mine. He outlined my lips with his tongue and then braced himself against the doorframe with his hands on my shoulders and kissed me until I was dizzy. He rubbed his rough hands up and down my arms until I shivered. If he hadn't had me firmly in his grasp I might have swooned. Israel Goodsend was definitely swoon worthy.

Breathless, I let out a sigh.

"Are you free on New Year's Eve?"

"I'm going home for the holidays, but I will be back in time for New Year's." I didn't tell him that I thought my ex was going to be in town, but Daniel hadn't formally asked me out for New Year's yet, and things were uncertain between us.

His mouth met mine again and teased my tongue. And *whoa!* Sparks flew. Was it because I was intoxicated, or that it had been a long season without? I wasn't going to dissect it now, not when Israel's hands were inches away from my—*whoa!* He was rubbing my skin with his fingers and getting deliciously close to my nipples, which were standing at attention. I wanted more of this, more of him. I reached my arms around his neck and returned his kisses. Four was certainly getting an eyeful. Should I invite him in? Crap, not when Four's car was idling in the parking lot.

"So you're free?"

"Yes," I answered in a rush.

"How about grabbing a movie next weekend?" he asked.

I wanted to grab something else, but thought better of it.

He went on, "I don't know if I can wait that long to see you again. How about dinner tomorrow night?"

"That sounds great."

A real date. Not a fix-up. I hadn't had one of those since I couldn't remember when. I was moving on with my life, and it felt exhilarating.

"I'll bet you've never been out on the town in Watertown."

"And you'd be right."

"Watertown is a hidden gem."

I had my doubts. "Where are we going?"

"I'll surprise you."

I liked surprises. Mostly everyone relied on me to do the planning. Frankly, I was tired of being the responsible one.

The next morning, I put in a full day's work and found that I enjoyed it, since I had an evening with Israel to look forward to. At five p.m., I locked my desk, and suddenly the director's body was hovering over mine.

"Going somewhere, Miss Saxe?"

I stiffened.

"You're not afraid of me, are you?"

Not afraid, exactly, but the man made me seriously nervous.

"You startled me, that's all. And I am going somewhere. Home."

"What if I said I wanted to talk about our *special project*?"

I was getting pretty tired of that phrase and all it insinuated.

"You were supposed to report to my office first thing this morning to talk about it. I've been waiting for you all day, and now you have me coming to you. I don't like to be kept waiting, Miss Saxe."

I inhaled a fortifying breath.

"Actually, I have a date tonight, so if you don't mind, I've got to leave now," I babbled. I looked around for help, but Peggy was on the phone, and Jean and Stanley had already gone.

The director smiled. "With Israel Goodspeed?"

"Yes." *Not that it's any of your business.*

"What is it between you and that Goodspeed boy?"

"He's not a boy. He's a man. And anyway, it's none of your business."

I grabbed my purse and got up from my seat.

The director held his hands up in mock defeat. "Okay, we'll resume our *conversation* bright and early in the morning. Be up at my office at eight thirty. And don't be late."

It half sounded like a threat. I ran out the door and didn't look back. I knew what the director was capable of, but I was more anxious to see Israel. And more than anxious to get out of range of the director. I truly didn't know what he wanted from me. I was already under his thumb and at his beck and call at work. Did he see me as a replacement bedmate for Savannah? I had already compromised my integrity by lying for him. What else was he looking for? I didn't feel like sticking around to find out.

Chapter Sixteen

"You look beautiful," Israel said, twirling me around in my flowing navy skirt, my white organic linen jersey tank under a round-necked cotton boucle top. Facing me, he gave me a sexy kiss. "It's a good thing we're going someplace fancy so I can show you off."

"Where are we having dinner?"

"You'll find out when we get there."

I crinkled my nose but I wasn't upset. I had spent time fixing my hair and wearing a flattering outfit, so it was nice to be appreciated. Anything to get my mind off both Daniel and the director.

We drove about fifteen minutes, which wasn't very far in Watertown. Israel stopped the car and parked in front of a Victorian mansion.

"Are we still in Watertown?"

"Just outside the city." He took my hand, and we walked to the entrance.

"The chef at this restaurant is from New York. The place just opened, and I've been wanting to try it. Some people at work have been here and rave about it. I hoped you might enjoy it."

"Thank you. I'm really looking forward to it." *And to being here with you.*

Israel looked almost good enough to eat in his navy suit and coordinating tie. I never would have imagined I would be taken to a fancy restaurant by such a handsome man when I first moved to Watertown. But here I was, living a dream, already infatuated with the man seated across from me at the table.

The restaurant could have been in any big city in the country. It was beautifully decorated. The wait staff was attentive, as was my date, and the food was varied and delicious.

I had pasta, of course, my favorite food—spaghetti carbonara—and it was delicious. Usually, I would never risk spaghetti in any restaurant but Italian, and even then, only a good Italian restaurant, but it was cooked just right. The bread was homemade and wonderful. I even had a glass of Moscato D'Asti, which was sweet, the way I liked it. And for dessert, a delicious key lime pie. Israel had a beautiful piece of Chilean sea bass, which he let me taste. Daniel never let me share his food.

"This is a fantastic restaurant, one of the best I've ever eaten in," I said, which for me was saying a lot. I was a bit of a food snob, but this restaurant met my standards and exceeded my expectations.

"So Watertown is not a complete disaster, then?" Israel posed.

"No, I have to admit it's growing on me."

"How about me? Am I growing on you?"

"Now I have two things to like about this town: this restaurant and you."

Israel beamed. "There's a lot more here to love, and I want to show you." He took my hand and stared into my eyes.

"I'd like that."

"So, Merritt Saxe, what are your plans for the

future? Do you plan to stay at the Division?"

I dropped his hand. "I want to stay for at least a year."

"And then what?" He sipped his coffee and lifted a forkful of tiramisu into his mouth.

I paused. "I don't know. I have no idea what I want to do with the rest of my life."

"What did you major in?"

"Journalism and criminology. I also took some creative writing courses."

"You could always write a book."

I finished off the remnants of my pie and the last of my peppermint tea.

"About what? They say you're supposed to write what you know. I haven't done anything worth writing about." Now, that wasn't exactly true. I was involved up to my neck in the biggest murder case the state had ever witnessed, but I *couldn't* write about that, or even talk about it.

"Hey, where did you go, there? You look a bit distracted."

"Just thinking about work. Wishing I didn't have to go back to it tomorrow."

"Do you have to?"

"We have a big press conference coming up, and I have a meeting with the director first thing in the morning."

"What if we played hooky?"

"I don't have enough time to just take off."

"Come on, call in sick."

"Then what would we do?"

"Play doctor?"

"You're a nut, you know that?"

113

"I've been called worse. C'mon, you obviously don't want to go back there. Tomorrow's Friday. We'll drive down the coast, have some great seafood, maybe stay overnight at a little bed and breakfast I know."

"Overnight? Isn't that moving a little too fast?"

"Is it?"

I blushed. Was it that obvious? If we weren't in public now, I'd be in his arms, right where I wanted to be. Daniel was a thousand miles away in every respect. And I wanted to be anywhere but at the office.

I guess he could tell I was ready to get intimate. He was probably used to girls falling all over him.

"If I had to guess, I'd bet you were the captain of your football team."

"Then you guessed right. And captain of the basketball team."

"I'm totally unathletic."

"It sounds like you're trying to find ways for me to dump you. In case you're wondering, it's not working."

I laughed. It felt good to laugh. "A bed and breakfast?"

"Separate rooms, if you insist."

"Well, then, Mr. Goodlove, I'll take you up on that offer."

"It's Good*speed*."

"Oops, I think I've had too much Asti."

"Don't let my name fool you. When I make love, I like to go slow."

All I could manage was a squeak.

"Well, we'd better go now if we want to get an early start tomorrow."

He helped me out of my chair and put his arm around me and steered me out of the restaurant.

When we got to my front door, I wondered if I should invite him in. I wanted to, but I could hardly stand up straight. The wine had gone right to my head. Israel folded me into his arms and just held me. It felt so good, so comfortable, so right being in his arms, and then he kissed me and I nearly melted into a puddle of mush.

"Merritt?" he whispered. "Are you asleep?"

"Mmm," I said, snuggling against him.

"Wake up, sleepyhead." He kissed me softly on the top of my head.

I stirred in his arms. "I must have fallen asleep standing up."

"You must have. I would suggest that I stay over to make sure you get to your bedroom, but that would be taking advantage. So until tomorrow? I'll pick you up at eight in the morning."

I got the keys out of my purse and opened the door. "Goodnight."

"Goodnight." And I did have a good night. Maybe the first good sleep I'd gotten since the murder. Dreaming of Israel Goodspeed.

Chapter Seventeen

My alarm woke me up at seven. I took a shower, got dressed, and picked up the phone.

"Jean," I croaked, not having to dissemble too much, since I was still hung over. "I woke up with a terrible headache and a cold. I don't want to get everyone sick. Will you tell Peggy for me? And I had an early meeting with the director. Will you please call and cancel? Tell him I'll be at his office first thing Monday morning. And thanks."

"Can I give him your number in case he wants to reach you?"

"I'd rather you not. I'm too sick to talk to anyone."

"Okay, get well soon. See you Monday."

I was really racking up the lies. Lying to the police, lying to my boss. I was getting really good at this. I applied my makeup carefully and spent time on my hair. I wanted to look great for our trip. I'd packed an overnight bag with a skimpy bathing suit and a cover-up, and some lace panties and a bra I'd bought to wear for Daniel. But Daniel was never going to see me in them. His loss. I threw in my birth control pills and a paperback romance novel, although I hoped to be too busy having a romance to read one.

Israel was right on time. *He's such a gentleman. So punctual. Always arrives when he says he will. I wonder what would happen if I brought him home. The conversation might go something like this: "So Mom, I'm dating this guy..."*

"Is he Jewish?"

"His name is Israel."

"Hmm. But is he Jewish?"

"Not exactly."

"What's his last name?"

"Goodspeed."

"Hmm."

My mother's "hmm" could mean any number of things. It could mean "Really?" or "What kind of name is Goodspeed?" or "Wait until your father hears about this." or "What happened to Daniel?" or "Are you kidding me?"

Actually, according to Israel, the name Goodspeed dated back to the Anglo-Saxon tribes of Britain and meant a person who performed good deeds and acts of kindness.

That said, religion would be a hurdle I would have to overcome. If it got that far. The fact that I had agreed to go out of town with him was a signal that it might go that far. I wasn't exactly used to going out of town with strange men. In fact, I had never been with a man other than Daniel.

"You look terrific," Israel said as he lifted my overnight bag and placed it in the trunk of his Jaguar.

"Thank you."

"Did you call in sick to work?"

"Yes, and I feel terrible about it. I had an appointment with the director this morning."

"From the way you say it, sounds like you weren't looking forward to it."

"I wasn't."

"Do you want to talk about it?"

"Not really."

"You can trust me."

"Your brother works for the director."

"I'm a lawyer."

"But I'm not your client."

"Do you need a lawyer?"

I hesitated. "I might."

"I'm here if you ever want to talk."

He helped me into the front seat.

"Well, Counselor, where are we going?"

"I thought we'd drive along the coast, get some lunch at a great seafood place I know. After that we can check into a neat bed and breakfast right on the beach and then just relax, sunbathe, and swim the rest of the day."

"That sounds heavenly."

As soon as the Gulf came into view, I really relaxed. By the time we got to the restaurant, I was starving. I had my usual, fried shrimp, with a baked potato and lemonade. Israel had the scallops.

"Wow, this shrimp is so tender and fresh."

"Shrimp is one of their specialties. It's one of my favorite places."

"Have you taken anyone else here, I mean any other girls?"

"No, you're the first." And the way he said it and the intensity of his gaze told me I might be the last.

I liked Israel. I liked him a lot. I intended to find out more about him on this little getaway.

Israel took care of the check, and we were off again.

"It's not too much longer. The beach at this place is

great, all white sand."

"I'm used to the brown sand—I think they refer to it as cinnamon—of the Atlantic."

"Right. I'm used to that hard-packed sand on Jax Beach. But this sand is like sugar, the way it slips through your fingers." Unsettled, I stared at his fingers.

About an hour later, we arrived at a quaint, Victorian-style B&B. It was painted green and white, and I fell in love with it. In the lobby were welcoming baskets of fresh apples, glasses of lemonade with sprigs of mint, and fresh zucchini muffins.

"Two rooms for Goodspeed."

"I'm afraid there's been a mistake, Mr. Goodspeed. We have you down for one room."

Israel looked genuinely upset. "But I requested two rooms."

The lady at the desk perused a card file. "We don't have any single rooms left, but I can give you the honeymoon suite. There's plenty of room for two people."

"How many beds?" I asked.

"Just one, but it's a king."

"Oh."

"I guarantee you'll be more than satisfied with the suite, Mrs. Goodspeed."

"Oh, I'm not—I mean—"

Israel turned to me, and I read the disappointment in his eyes. "We can try another place."

"No, the honeymoon suite will be fine," I assured the lady.

"No extra charge." She smiled.

"Well, then, we'll take it."

She handed Israel the keys, and he handed me my

own key.

"The valet will bring up your luggage directly. And meanwhile, feel free to enjoy the amenities. We'll have dinner in the dining room at seven."

Israel took my hand, and we rode the elevator to the fifth floor.

"I'm sorry, I really did reserve two single rooms. I can sleep on the couch."

When we entered the honeymoon suite, I was dazzled. The room was spacious and well-appointed. There was a lovely view of the ocean from every window.

"You have nothing to be sorry about. This is great."

"I'm glad you like it."

Just then the valet arrived and arranged our luggage on the luggage racks. He placed a bottle of Champagne to cool in an ice bucket. "Compliments of the manager."

"Thank you," Israel said, and tipped the valet generously.

I twirled around the room. "I can't believe we got the honeymoon suite."

"My brother and I came here once with my parents, and I thought I'd like to bring my wife back here one day on our honeymoon."

"That's very romantic," I said.

"Looks like my dream came true, Mrs. Goodspeed."

While I was trying that name out for size, Israel suggested we change into our bathing suits.

"The beach really is beautiful," he said.

I changed in the bathroom, which was probably the

size of a regular single room, and Israel changed in the bedroom.

We rode the elevator down, and when we got to the beach, Israel paid a guy to set up chairs under an umbrella.

"You think of everything."

"I try."

Two fluffy monogrammed white towels lay on the table next to the chairs.

"It's unseasonably warm today. I think it's warm enough to swim," Israel said. "I'll race you to the water."

We ran to the water and waded in.

"This water is great. I love the white sand. I could stay in here all day."

We swam around. I floated. The waves knocked us down, and we finally made our way back to our lounge chairs. Israel handed me a signature towel from the table, and I dried off.

"This place has everything."

"It does now that you're here," he said.

We lay in our lounges and drowsed in the sun like loopy dragonflies for what seemed like hours. Periodically, a server came over and took our drink orders. I must have gone through three sugary concoctions, each with a floating umbrella and a cherry.

Israel took my hand in his much broader one. It felt warm and wonderful. He kept rubbing his thumb suggestively over the flesh of my hand, and I had to concentrate not to explode in orgasmic delight. Maybe it was the three drinks. Or maybe it was the sun. But maybe it was the man. He erased all thoughts of Savannah Braddock, the director, and Daniel.

"This has been the best day," I whispered.

"It's not over yet," he promised.

I shivered.

"Are you getting cold? We can go inside. We need to shower and change for dinner. The food here is great."

We got up reluctantly and walked through the lobby to the elevators.

When we got to our room, there were two bottles of water on the dresser. We hadn't even touched the Champagne yet.

"You shower first," he offered.

What I wanted to do was shower with him. I felt so naughty I almost voiced my innermost thoughts.

I grabbed the signature robe from the closet and the complimentary bedroom slippers and walked into the bathroom. This bathroom had everything. It was stocked with Moulton Brown body wash, shampoo and conditioner, a yellow loofah, and body lotion. My body was longing for Israel's, but I knew he was too much of a gentleman to barge in. I rubbed my hands over my body and imagined they were Israel's hands. Then I got down to business washing my hair. I took out the hair dryer and walked out in my robe to plug the dryer into the outlet near the table.

"All yours," I said.

He looked at me with a hunger in his eyes like he was taking my words literally.

I walked away and started drying my hair. I was dressed by the time he got out of the shower and dressed in the bathroom. Long, tall, and gorgeous, he'd changed into slacks, a white long-sleeved shirt, and a sports coat.

He looked me over appreciatively. "You look stunning."

"Thanks."

He took my arm, and we walked down to the dining room together. As we were being seated, Israel told me he had made arrangements to have our Champagne uncorked to enjoy with the meal.

The server handed us the menus. There was a nice selection to choose from. I was dying for the lobster, but it was so pricey. I swear that man could read my mind.

"I'm having the lobster. It's really superb here, if you'd like to try it. Don't worry, I can afford it."

I blushed.

"The lady and I will have the lobster, with a baked potato, and what is the vegetable of the day?"

"Green beans, sir."

I nodded.

"Then we'll have that. And please pour the Champagne."

Israel was right. The dinner was delicious, and the Champagne was definitely going to my head. We each had a different decadent dessert.

By the time we walked to the room, Israel had to hold me up.

"Sorry, but I think I'm a little tipsy."

"You're a lightweight. Can't hold your liquor. I'll remember that. No worries. I've got you."

He unlocked the door, and I threw my purse down on the dresser, peeled off my clothes down to the bra and underwear, and flopped face first onto the bed, which the bed-and-breakfast fairy had turned back. Israel stood over me and covered me.

"Have a good sleep. I'll be on the couch."

I turned over and pulled him down to the bed.

"Come to bed, silly."

"I don't think that's a good idea," he said. "Me and you in bed together, I might get ideas."

"I like ideas."

"But you're not yourself."

"Who do you think I am?"

"You've had too much to drink. I don't want to take advantage. I don't want you to have any regrets."

"And you have too many clothes on, Mr. Goodspeed. If you don't touch me right now, I'm going to explode. Where's Mr. Yummy?"

"Mr.Yummy?"

I smiled and batted my eyelashes, not realizing I'd just let him know my pet name for him and his sidekick.

"Are you sure?"

I nodded my head and opened my arms. I'd never been so sure of anything in my life. I had only just met him, but somehow I knew we were meant to be together. I knew I wanted this.

Israel didn't waste another minute. He probably set a new world record for getting naked. When he came into my arms, he unhooked my bra and filled his hands with my breasts.

"Oh, God, Merritt, you are so beautiful." He kissed me and deepened the kiss and I felt it right down to my toes. I wriggled in his arms restlessly. I was trying to get my panties off, but I couldn't seem to find them. I needn't have worried. Israel to the rescue. He placed his broad hands on the waistband of my panties and slipped them down slowly.

Now it was just his body on top of mine. He felt right there. I felt safe. I felt loved.

He moved his hands lower and touched me and tortured me. I wanted him to take me right then.

Again, we were on the same wavelength. Israel was reading my mind.

"Not so fast, Miss Saxe," he said in a measured voice. "I want you to scream my name."

I moaned. "Oh God, Israel."

"Louder, sweetheart."

"Israel," I pleaded.

"Louder, darlin'."

I pouted, and he planted quick kisses on my lips. "I can't hear you."

"I can't talk with your lips on mine," I mumbled.

"Do you want me to stop?"

I felt him smile against my mouth.

"No!"

Then his mouth went lower.

"Take me now," I screamed.

He plunged into my body with such force that it knocked the breath out of me. I clung to him as he kept up the torture. I gave as good as I got and called out his name again.

When it was over, he collapsed onto my stomach. He was still inside me.

"Oh, God," I whispered.

"Is that a good *Oh, God* or a bad *Oh, God*?"

"Couldn't you tell? That was the best sex I've ever had." And it was. I didn't know whether it was because of the Champagne, which I wasn't used to drinking, or the memory of the sun on my body, or that sex with Israel was new and exciting. Or because Israel was so different from Daniel. Or because I was falling in love with Israel and out of love with Daniel. Whatever the reason, I was more satisfied than I'd ever been, and happier.

He laughed and gave me a chaste kiss. "You slayed me, Merritt."

I smiled a naughty smile. "I think Mr. Yummy is dead."

"Mr. Yummy?"

I blushed and touched him where he immediately sprang to life.

"Christ, Merritt. You don't know what you're doing to me."

"Oh, I think I do."

"So you want to play dirty? Two can play at this game. Apparently, Mr. Yummy is very much alive and ready for an encore." He pulled out and checked. "Yep."

"Are you kidding?"

"No, Mr. Yummy has a lot of staying power. Are you up for another round?"

I sighed contentedly and took him into my arms. I felt his body with my hands. I wanted to touch every part of him, and I wanted him back inside me. When he obliged, Mr. Yummy was rock hard. "Israel Goodspeed, you are amazing."

"No, Merritt Saxe, you're the amazing one. I love you."

I didn't think I heard that right. Maybe I was dreaming.

"I couldn't hear you, Mr. Goodspeed."

"I said, I love you."

"Louder," I teased.

"I love you," he shouted.

This was a night to remember. With Israel, I wasn't shy about asking for what I wanted, and Israel wasn't shy about giving it to me. But it wasn't just about sex. It was more. It felt bigger, more important. Something wonderful was happening between us. Sated, I fell into a deep sleep, the most restful sleep I'd had in a long time.

The next morning we were coiled around each other in the king bed. Mr. Yummy was stirring.

"So, sleepyhead. How do you feel?"

"I've never felt so well-used, so relaxed."

"How much do you remember about last night?"

"It's all sort of foggy."

"Oh, it is, is it? Do you remember Mr. Yummy?"

"Mr. Yummy?" Had I called out my nickname for Israel in my sleep? How embarrassing.

He took Mr. Yummy out of hiding. "Exhibit A."

I hid my head in Israel's stomach.

"Don't be embarrassed." He took my chin in his hands. "Look at me."

I turned away.

"You have nothing to be embarrassed about. What we did last night was intimate, and beautiful. Do you remember what I told you?"

"You told me a lot of things."

"Specifically, I told you I loved you. And I didn't say it in the heat of the moment. I'm in love with you, Merritt Saxe."

"How can you be so sure? We hardly know each other."

"Because I've never felt this way about anyone before."

I disentangled myself from Israel and propped my back against the headboard.

"You've never had a girlfriend?"

"Sure I have. But I've never said that to anyone else."

"You were never serious with a girl?"

"I've come close but never said the words. That was the undoing of several relationships."

"Your lack of commitment?"

"I was never ready before. You told me that's pretty much what happened with your old boyfriend."

"After dating for four years, I just assumed we were going to get married. But then he started law school, and he wouldn't make a commitment. I didn't want to wait three more years without it."

"Lucky for me. Did you love him?"

"Yes, I thought I did."

"What do you mean?"

"I mean we said it to each other. I slept with him, so of course I thought I was in love. But it turns out I didn't know what love was."

Israel looked puzzled.

I took his hand in mine. "I didn't believe it could happen this fast. I mean we practically just met, but I am falling in love with you. What came before doesn't even compare."

He tightened his grip on my hand. "Thank you for saying that. Are you planning to see him when you go home over the holidays?"

"He called and wants to see me. I had asked him to come to Watertown with me. But that was before, before you."

"Will you let him?"

"Not now. I will have to hear what he has to say."

"What if he gets you a ring?"

"If he does, it will be only because he feels pressured. Are you jealous?"

"Completely," Israel admitted. "I've just met you. He's had four years with you."

"I know. It doesn't make sense, but I've never felt the way I feel around you. I'm powerless to do anything about it."

"I know you had too much to drink last night. I was afraid you might wake up with regrets the morning after."

"I knew exactly what I was doing. I wanted you."

Israel blew out a breath, wrapped his arms around me, and just held me.

I smiled. I felt deliriously happy. "Let's check out the famous breakfast you were telling me about. I'm starving."

"You're going to love it. I promise."

"So far I've loved everything about this trip. And we still have all day today."

"And tonight," he added.

"And then back to reality."

"Merritt, you know you can tell me anything. Something is obviously weighing on you."

"You're very perceptive, Counselor. And I do feel like I can trust you with anything. But right now I have things under control."

Israel didn't look convinced. "But promise you'll come to me if you need help."

"I will."

The rest of the day was as marvelous as the day before. We enjoyed the wonderful breakfast, we walked the beach, collected shells, sunbathed, showered *together*, and did some shopping. Then we stopped in a little seafood shack that had delicious fried shrimp and creamy clam chowder.

That night we made love again, but this time the pace was slower. I felt seriously cherished by this new man in my life. And I came to the realization that Israel was indeed a man, compared to Daniel. Daniel was a college crush, but Israel Goodspeed was the real thing. And then there was the incomparable Mr. Yummy.

Israel dropped me off at my apartment late Sunday night.

"Thank you for a wonderful weekend," I said.

"I was about to say the same thing to you. I can't wait to see you again. I'll pick you up right after work and we'll grab some dinner, maybe see a movie."

"You are sweeping me off my feet, Mr. Goodspeed."

"I have a lot of time to make up for. I love you, Merritt." He sealed it with a kiss.

"I know." I didn't say it back. It was too new. But I did feel it.

Chapter Eighteen

"Miss Saxe. Are you avoiding me?"

I was seated in a chair directly across from the director, in the proverbial hot seat.

I cleared my throat. "No." The director was a man of few words. I could play the same game. "Didn't Jean tell you I called in sick Friday?"

"Strange. Then you must be overheated, or else your sunburn is turning into a nice tan. I'm sorry you were cooped up in the house all weekend. Evidently, you've made a miraculous recovery. By the way, how are you and Israel Goodspeed doing?"

"That's personal. It's none of your business."

"Everything you do is my business, Miss Saxe. There's something different about you. I can't quite put my finger on it."

I blushed, became sullen, and then angry.

"Are you having me followed?"

"Do I need to? You're not afraid of me, are you, Miss Saxe?"

I stood up. "I'm just annoyed. I think this cat-and-mouse game you're playing with me has gone on long enough. I'm sorry I ever picked you up that morning. I wish I hadn't seen what I saw. I just want to forget about the whole thing. And for you to leave me alone. I don't want to be any part of this."

"Sit down, Miss Saxe," he scolded. "Unfortunately,

you are very much a part of it. Your livelihood is in my hands, and so is your fate. So I would suggest we get on with our business."

Somehow, I thought, what the director said and the influence he was trying to exert on me was illegal, or at least improper, or if it wasn't, it should be.

"And exactly what is our business?"

"We are going to meet periodically so there will be a record that we are working together on a very important project. You are penciled in on my calendar."

"I'm your alibi. We're not working on any project. And I don't want to be here."

"Ah, there's that spunk I knew was in there. Miss Saxe, you're very much mistaken if you think you have a choice in the matter. You will sit down, and we will stay in here for the next hour until our business is settled."

I sat down and scowled. Inside, I was boiling mad. This man was a bully, but he had the heft of the entire division behind him. He could make people go away. He'd already killed one person. Who knew what else he'd done?

"Merritt," he said, gently. "You still think I killed Savannah. I told you before, I loved her. She was pregnant with my child. I would never have harmed her."

"Maybe you did love her. But maybe that child was an issue. Maybe Miss Braddock was going to go to your wife. You couldn't have Miss Julia finding out about your affair."

"You don't know what you're talking about."

"I've seen your temper. I know what you're capable of."

"Your insubordination is distressing, Miss Saxe. On your way out, tell my secretary to hold my calls, and you be in my office first thing tomorrow morning."

I stood up abruptly. I couldn't wait to leave his office. I couldn't stand the sight of him. It was like he was punishing me. Things couldn't continue this way. But how could I get out of his clutches?

"Oh, and Miss Saxe, give my regards to Mr. Goodspeed when you see him again tonight."

Alarmed, I faced the door so he couldn't see the expression on my face. The director was having me followed...or else he was using Israel to do his dirty work. Of course. How stupid could I be? How could Israel have fallen in love with me so quickly? He couldn't have. I should have known the relationship was too good to be true. He was working for the director all this time. And I had fallen for it. I had slept with the enemy. I was nothing more than a slut. Worse than that, I was a predictable slut, sleeping with the first man who paid attention to me after my breakup. How pathetic.

I slammed the door and swept past his secretary. I wasn't going to make another appointment. I wasn't going to come to the director's office like a pawn in his twisted game. I was through with him. And I was going to give Israel Goodspeed, if that was even his real name, a piece of my mind and end this farce of a relationship tonight. I wanted to put Mr. Yummy and his namesake through a meat grinder and grind his balls to paste.

The director knew I had broken up with Daniel. So he got his friend's brother to bait the trap. In my head, I replayed the scene and all the things I did with Israel in that great big bed, all the things I'd said. By now he and his brother and the director were having a good laugh at my expense.

I got to my office, and Jean told me Peggy was looking for me.

"I told her you were in the director's office, and she went ballistic."

"Jean, listen to me. There's been a family emergency. I have to go back to Miami."

"But we're having the Tent City press conference. Peggy needs you."

"You and Stanley can handle it. I need to leave right away."

I bolted out of the office before Jean could respond.

I drove back to my apartment, threw some things into a suitcase, and began driving. My first reflex was to call Israel to let him know I wouldn't be in town for our date, but I didn't owe him anything. I wanted to have it out with him, but right now all I wanted to do was go home to Miami. Daniel wouldn't be home from school for a few days, but that's where I needed to be. I had told Israel that what I felt for Daniel was not real love, but apparently I didn't know the difference. Israel was just using me. It had all started when Peggy fixed me up for the holiday party. Maybe Peggy was in on The Big Conspiracy too.

Chapter Nineteen

"Merritt?"

"Hi, Daniel. When did you get home?"

"Just now. I'm going to spend some time with my family, and then I want to take you out to Sarucci's, if you're still speaking to me."

"I guess I am speaking to you. That sounds nice."

I showered and put on the new dress I'd just bought in The Gables on Miracle Mile. It was expensive but very flattering and in my favorite color—green. When I saw it on the rack, I knew I had to have it. Money would be tight when I quit my job, but I was determined to find another job in Miami. I'd just have to learn to speak Spanish.

I told my parents I was homesick and that was the reason I left Watertown. They were thrilled to have me home again, so they didn't ask questions. I'd spent most of the week pining over Israel, but in my heart I knew he was falsehearted. I berated myself about being such a fool. I hadn't had any contact with Peggy or Jean—or blessedly, the director. I supposed they knew where I was from my personnel file, but as long as I wasn't in Watertown causing trouble, they would be satisfied.

When I heard Daniel's voice, I got a little wistful. We'd had four years of wonderful memories. I could convince myself I was still in love with him. I'd have to reserve judgment until I saw him again.

When I did, my heart didn't do the flip it did when I'd laid my eyes on Israel. It didn't skip a beat. He was familiar, dear even, but my spirit didn't soar. He hugged me and somehow he seemed diminished, less than he was before. I would wait to hear what he had to say. He approached me shyly, trying to gauge my reaction, and then he kissed me. Sparks didn't fly. I didn't want to jump into bed with him like I had in Charlottesville, but still, it was Daniel.

"I missed you," he began.

I didn't say anything in response but asked, "How were your finals?"

"I think I did okay. I was a wreck thinking about us."

I was silent.

"You're going to make this difficult, aren't you?"

I shrugged.

"Let's get to the restaurant, or we'll miss our reservation."

Good old Daniel. He was committed to getting to the restaurant on time, just not to spending a lifetime with me.

"How's work?" he asked.

"I'd rather not talk about it. I don't think I'm going back."

"Did something go wrong?"

"You could say that, but let's talk about that later."

We arrived at the restaurant, and the owner had reserved our favorite table at our favorite place. "Welcome back," he said effusively. "My two favorite people."

"Thank you, Silvio," I said, hugging him.

"Tonight, on this special occasion, I am going to

personally take your order."

What special occasion?

He winked at Daniel. "I have some complimentary focaccia coming to the table." He signaled, and a server brought over a plate. "Now how about some drinks?"

Daniel ordered a glass of Merlot.

"Nothing for me, thank you," I said, remembering what happened the last time I had too much to drink.

"No amaretto sour?" Silvio asked.

"Not right now," I answered, preferring to see how the evening progressed. I needed to concentrate.

"I know you two know the menu by heart. We have some specials, but I already know what you're going to order. So what shall I bring you?"

"I'll have spaghetti carbonara," I said.

"And bring me the lasagna," said Daniel.

He nodded. "Coming right up." He gave Daniel another meaningful look.

"What is going on between the two of you?" I asked.

"I just told him to make this a special night. So what are you going to do if you quit your job?"

"Try to get a job here."

"I thought you hated Miami."

"It's better than Watertown."

"Maybe there's another alternative."

"Like what?"

"Like moving to Charlottesville."

"Charlottesville? Why would I want to do that?"

"That's all you talked about last semester."

"There's no reason for me to move there."

"What about me?"

"What about you?"

"Us, Merritt. I thought you wanted to be together."

"There is no us, Daniel."

"Let's table that discussion. Here comes Silvio with the drinks."

"Merlot for the gentleman and Champagne for the lady." He placed a glass of Champagne in front of me.

"I didn't order this."

"It's on the house."

I didn't want to seem ungracious, though I didn't want to drink Champagne. "Thank you."

I picked up the goblet and was about to drink when I noticed a shadow at the bottom of the glass.

"There's something in my glass, Silvio. Could you bring me another one?"

"Maybe you ought to look closer, signorina." Grinning, he walked away.

I stared into the fizzy liquid. Something was sparkling at the bottom of the glass.

Daniel took the glass and fished around the bottom. He lifted something from the glass. "Look what I found."

I stared at it. It was a ring. It looked like an engagement ring.

"Aren't you going to say anything?" He dropped the ring into my hand.

What was I supposed to say? I stared dumbly at the ring in my hand.

"Merritt, it's an engagement ring. I'm asking you to marry me."

I froze as the chilled Champagne dripped through my fingers.

"Isn't it what you wanted? I didn't want to lose you."

"You can't afford this ring. It's beautiful, but—"

"My parents helped me out. I told them about what happened, and they agreed we should be together."

"Are you saying you want to marry me, now?"

"Not now. I'm still a one-L. But we'd be engaged, and when I finish law school—"

"In three years."

"Yes, in three years, then I would get a job and we'd get married. But in the meantime, you could move to Charlottesville and get a job."

That would solve one of my problems. Getting away from Watertown, from the murder, from the director. I wasn't worried about getting a job. Maybe it wouldn't be in my profession, but I would take any job. At least that's what I had convinced myself. But I enjoyed working in my field. I didn't want to be with Daniel enough to give that up.

"Merritt?"

"I didn't expect this."

"I wanted it to be a surprise."

"It's a shock, really. I mean, we were broken up. There's been no communication between us, and now you give me a ring?"

"Do you want me to get down on one knee?" He proceeded to do just that. Everyone in the restaurant was staring at us in anticipation.

I looked—really looked—at Daniel. It would be the easiest, most natural thing to say, "Yes," to use Daniel as my ticket out. Eventually, if I was out of sight, the director would forget about me. He'd realize I wasn't going to cause trouble. He'd loosen his hold on me. But I owed Daniel the truth. Not about the murder. The fewer people who knew the truth about that the better. But marriage was a big step. A step I was not ready to take. Not with Daniel. Not now that I knew what love could be like. Even though I knew it wasn't real.

"Daniel, I can't accept this. I don't want to marry you."

The look of surprise, then shock, signaled that he was crestfallen. I think I'll remember that look for the rest of my life.

"But I thought... You said... Didn't you want—" He started to get up.

Suddenly, we were surrounded by the wait staff, and Silvio danced over singing, congratulating us effusively, and placing two steaming hot dishes of food in front of us. The restaurant patrons were clapping. It was a nightmare.

"Stop," Daniel shouted. "Go away."

When Silvio's face registered confusion, Daniel said simply, "She didn't say yes."

The celebrators faded into the background. The well-wishers went back to their dinners, looking down at their menus and furtively out of the corners of their eyes to find out what had precipitated this disaster.

"Aren't you going to eat your lasagna?" I asked, putting the ring down on the tablecloth and pushing it toward Daniel.

"I've lost my appetite," he said. He picked up the ring and pushed it back toward me. "I want you to keep it. Just promise me you'll think about it. I know I blindsided you. You weren't expecting it. It's an important decision. You need to think about what you want to do."

I frowned. What I really wanted to do was to pick

up my fork and dig into my spaghetti carbonara. Why did I turn Daniel down when just a few weeks ago there was nothing I wanted more than to become his wife? Why, because I'd fallen in love with and slept with Israel Goodspeed. But Israel Goodspeed was a phantom. That relationship wasn't real. I owed Daniel the courtesy of thinking, really thinking, about his proposal. I took the ring, wrapped it in a paper napkin, and placed it in the zipper pocket of my purse.

"Okay, I'll think about it. And thank you." I was a coward, delaying the inevitable. It wouldn't hurt any less if I declined his proposal in another day or a week.

"This isn't how I thought the evening would go."

"Eat your lasagna," I said, twirling a forkful of carbonara into a spoon.

Chapter Twenty

After a perfunctory goodnight kiss, Daniel drove away, downcast and disappointed. I went to unlock the door with my key and ran right into my mother.

"You've got company."

Could this night get any weirder? I didn't want to see anyone. I just wanted to go to bed.

"He says his name is Israel and that he knows you."

My senses were on high alert. Israel here? He had followed me to my house!

"Your dad is already asleep," said my mother, walking down the hall to her bedroom. "I'll leave you two alone. It was nice to meet you, Israel," she added.

"You too, Mrs. Saxe, and thank you for the brisket. It was delicious."

"You gave him dinner?"

"He arrived right after you left. He drove all that way. I had to feed the boy."

Jeesh. My own mother was betraying me.

I turned an accusatory face to Israel. "What are you doing here?"

"I was frantic. You weren't at home when I came to pick you up for our date. I called your office the next morning, and they said you had a family emergency. I was worried sick, but they wouldn't give me your home phone number. I finally had my brother sweet talk

Peggy into giving him your address. I drove all day to get here. It turns out everyone in your family is fine. So what's up? Why did you just leave without letting me know?"

"Because you're not the boss of me."

Israel laughed. "You know you sound like a spoiled little brat. I'd shake you senseless, but I'm so relieved. I was scared something had happened to you. Or to someone in your family. I wanted to be here for you. I thought I might never see you again. I think you owe me an explanation."

"I didn't ask you to come."

"I know that. Merritt, what's wrong?"

I rounded on him. "Don't act all innocent. I know who you are and what you've been doing. So don't bother pretending that you care."

"What are you talking about? Of course I care. I wouldn't be here if I didn't."

"The jig is up. I figured it out. You're the director's little lap dog, and your job is to spy on me and report back to the director. Whose idea was it to sleep with me? Yours or his? You both make me sick. I want you to leave. And you can tell your best bud, the director, I'm not coming back to Watertown."

"Merritt, you're not making any sense. What are you talking about? I don't even know the director. I met him briefly that one time at the party at his house."

"You expect me to believe you?"

"Why wouldn't you?"

"Just go back to Watertown. I'm not interested in anything you have to say."

"Merritt, did you forget what we have? What we found together?"

I laughed and added a snarky, "Ha! You used me in the worst way. You made me fall in love with you. And I'm never going to forgive you. I don't know how you can live with yourself."

"Stop this. Please, tell me what I'm missing. I don't understand any of this. I love you, Merritt. And I know you love me."

I shook my head, fished my hand into my purse and unwrapped the napkin. Then I took the ring and placed it on my finger.

"What is that?" he demanded.

"That," I stated, "is an engagement ring. I'm engaged to Daniel Krantz. So you can just move along."

"When did this happen?"

"Tonight, and we're very happy."

"I thought you loved me."

"How can I love someone who lies to me? Who sleeps with me to keep me contained and compliant? Who associates with murderers?"

"Murderers? I don't have any idea what you're talking about. If you're in love with your ex-boyfriend, I get that. If that's what you want…" He shrugged. "But please, help me to understand. I thought what we shared was real."

"I thought so too. But it wasn't. So just go."

Israel grabbed me by my shoulders and yanked me down onto the couch, where he sat next to me. "Now, young lady, you are going to tell me what's going on right now, or I'm going to put you over my lap and spank you."

I choked. "You're going to do what?" I pummeled him with my hands and tried to break free.

"You're not getting away until you tell me what is wrong. I'm stronger than you. I'm prepared to stay all night. You know I have *staying power*. Now we're either going to get to the bottom of this or I'm going to wallop that plump little bottom of yours."

"You bastard," I sputtered. "You wouldn't dare. Let me go."

"Okay, you asked for it." He heaved me over his lap and began spanking.

"I'll scream."

Israel clamped his hand over my mouth and spanked me with his other hand. "Do your best."

"Gurk, damn," I seethed through his fingers.

"What did you say?"

"Bast," I mumbled.

"Can I just say this hurts me more than it hurts you?"

I kicked and squirmed, but he held me firmly against his lap and continued spanking me. It started as a punishment and then turned into something else when he suggestively massaged my bottom to soothe the sting of each smack.

I was furious. I was also getting turned on. The bastard.

"And may I just say that dress is killer on you. I'm going to enjoy taking it off."

"You wouldn't dare!" I managed.

"What was that you said? That you love me? I couldn't quite hear you. Louder, sweetheart."

I kept up the struggle, but that seemed to excite him even more. I could tell by the way Mr. Yummy was making his presence known. My nipples tightened. When I got free, I was going to beat the bastard until he was black and blue. I was going to bite him, scratch him, then strangle him. I wanted him to turn me over and kiss me.

I let out a loud sob. A frustrated bleat, actually.

Sensing my distress, he turned me over and pressed me tenderly to his body until I went limp in his arms. "Merritt, sweetheart, have I hurt you? Please, don't cry. I just needed to know what was wrong. I never meant to hurt you." He kissed my eyes and tasted the salty tears. I hated, hated, hated him, and at the same time I wanted him more than ever. I was all over the place. When he moved his lips to kiss mine, I reached my arms around his neck and returned the kiss with abandon.

I hung on for dear life, crying and hiccupping.

"It's all right. I'm here. Now tell me everything."

And I did. From the way he reacted, I realized he was not involved. At the same time, he couldn't believe what I was telling him.

"Did you actually see him kill Judge Braddock?"

"I walked in after it was over. There was blood all over him and all over the place. There was a bloody knife sticking out of her belly. She was pregnant, for God's sake. He killed his own child."

"Are you sure about that?"

"Who else could have done it?"

"Did he admit it?"

"He says he's innocent, that he loved her."

"I'm not a criminal lawyer, but maybe he deserves the benefit of the doubt. And the fact that you've held back critical information makes you an accessory. Let me go and talk to him."

"It's too dangerous. If he killed once, he can kill again. He'd do anything to shut me up. He gave me a promotion I didn't deserve, after all."

"Well, he sounds like a very dangerous man."

I punched his iron-tight stomach. "You think this is funny?"

"I'm not laughing. If he did this, then he needs to be punished."

"That's not going to happen. He has the power of the division behind him. He has powerful friends, even in the police force. They came to his office. I was there."

"What happened when you were questioned?"

"He implied that he and I were…that I was his mistress, and that I was with him at the time of the murder." Israel's muscles tightened.

"He forced me to sign a false statement."

"He forced you?"

"He made it clear I was to follow orders or else."

"Or else what?"

"I didn't want to find out. I knew what he was capable of. I didn't want to end up like Savannah Braddock. I lied, Israel."

"That's bad, but you were under duress." Israel thought for a moment. "Here's what we're going to do. We're going to go back to Watertown and confront him. I'll give him a chance to explain himself. I want you to write everything down the way you remember it. We're going to have that ready in case something should happen to one of us. It's our insurance policy."

"You see, you do believe he's dangerous."

"I believe he could be. He might do anything to protect himself. When you accused him of murder, what did he say in his defense?"

"He just said he loved her and would never kill her.

But he doesn't give another explanation. He said he gave the police the files of some inmates who had a grudge against Savannah."

"Round up the usual suspects, like in *Casablanca.*"

"Exactly."

"Well, you're not alone in this anymore. Do you have a dollar?"

"A dollar?"

"Yes. My legal fee. From now on, I represent you." I got a dollar out of my wallet and handed it to him.

"And now, get it off your mind. We have better things to do."

"I doubt you can get a hotel at this time of night. Why don't you sleep here on the couch?"

"Your mother already invited me to stay the night. My things are in the guest room."

"My mother? Does she know you're not Jewish?"

"No, but I used the magic word."

"And what is that?"

"Israel."

I shook my head and smiled. "That won't last long when she finds out you're not really Jewish."

"I had a good conversation with your dad."

"What did you two talk about?"

"The Holy Roman Empire."

I nodded. "Dad was a history teacher before he started selling insurance."

"Right. He said, 'Son, the first thing you have to know about the Holy Roman Empire is that it's not holy, it's not Roman, and it's not an empire.' Then he tried to sell me an insurance policy."

"Jeesh. I'm sorry."

"I like them."

"Well, look. I'm pretty beat. Did my mom show you where the towels are?"

"She did. I'm all set."

"Well, then, I guess I'll see you in the morning."

"Oh, you'll see me way before that." Israel lifted me off the couch. "Show me the way to your bedroom."

"You're not sleeping in my room. Not with my parents in the house."

"Your mother made it a point to say that they are heavy sleepers."

"I don't know what to say to that."

"I've always imagined what it would be like to sleep with you in your childhood bedroom. Naughty and sexy."

"Careful, Counselor, your halo is slipping."

"Where is it?" he said, huffing and puffing, feigning exhaustion, while I felt weightless in his arms.

"Turn right here," I instructed.

He carried me through the bedroom door and placed me on my bed.

Then he walked over and locked the door.

He came back to the bed and started to strip.

"Now take it off."

"Take what off?"

"That ring. I'm not sleeping with you until you take off that poser's ring."

I fingered the ring. "I haven't made up my mind yet."

"Well, if you have, I intend to change it."

I removed the ring and placed it on the nightstand. "We need to be very quiet. I don't want my parents to hear."

"I can do quiet. Can you? We're going to take it

nice and slow, baby."

I shivered. There was much more to Israel Goodspeed than met the eye. I believed him. I believed in him. I believed in us.

He turned off the light and turned toward me, and I was more than ready for him.

Chapter Twenty-One

The next day we drove back to Watertown. It was a six-hour drive, and Israel followed me in his car. He didn't want to waste time. He was going to come with me to my meeting with the director.

"But you've missed so much work already," I protested.

"You're much more important than work."

I had a feeling Israel Goodspeed would have tanked his law school finals for me. He was not afraid of commitment or confrontation. And that is just what this early morning meeting with the director was going to be all about. Confronting the enemy.

Naturally, I was scared. But it felt good to have backup. Israel had alerted his brother, who offered to drive from Jacksonville for the meeting.

"Not necessary. I just want someone else to know about this, just in case," he told his brother. His brother couldn't believe what Israel told him. Despite his allegiance to the director, family loyalty prevailed. He was definitely on Israel's side, which meant he was on my side.

We walked up to the director's office. His secretary, who did not like me at all but couldn't take her eyes off Israel, said, "The director is ready for you, Merritt." She turned her attention to Israel. "His appointment is with Miss Saxe." Glancing back at me, she asked, "Who is this man?"

"He's my lawyer"—*and my lover*, I wanted to add—"Israel Goodspeed," I said in my most hands-off voice.

"Any relation to Four?"

"He's my brother."

"Then you can go in."

We walked into the lion's den. The director was sitting in his chair. His coat was off, and his muscles were bulging out of his starched blue shirt. Next he would probably flex them. He was shooting daggers at Israel. But Israel was not intimidated. There was so much testosterone in the room, I thought it might implode.

"Miss Saxe."

"Director."

We started our usual verbal dance.

"Aren't you Four's brother? You came with Merritt to my holiday party. What are you doing here?"

"I'm Miss Saxe's attorney. She has retained me to assist her during this difficult time."

"What the hell have you gone and done, Merritt?" he brayed. "I'm very disappointed. I thought we had an agreement."

I stepped back and bumped right into Israel. He placed a reassuring hand on my back to steady me.

"I am speaking for Miss Saxe at this meeting. As I said, I will be negotiating on her behalf."

My legs were as shaky as a newborn fawn's, and my stomach was tied in knots. Israel sensed that I needed to sit, led me to a seat, and took a seat beside me.

"First, I would like to inform you that Miss Saxe

has written a detailed letter, a statement of sorts, outlining everything that took place on the morning of Savannah Braddock's murder, so that in the event anything should happen to either Miss Saxe or myself, that letter would be sent to the Watertown police department and all of the state newspapers, and a copy would go to your wife."

The director seethed. "Leave my wife out of this. You're bluffing, Goodspeed. Merritt Saxe has already filed a sworn statement about her whereabouts on the morning of the murder. She was with me, at my house, working on a special project. If she were to change her story, she would be held in contempt."

"And you would be accused of murder."

"So we have a stand-off."

Israel, as cool as a cucumber under pressure, shook his head. "I don't think you understand all the ramifications of your situation, Director. Miss Saxe was under duress when she signed that statement. She is an employee of yours, and in her subordinate position, you exercised undue influence over her. You broke any number of laws with your actions. She would not be held accountable. But you would."

"You can't do this."

"We can and we did."

"Who else did you tell?" the director asked Israel but was looking directly at me.

"I told my brother."

"I told Merritt I didn't kill Savannah Braddock."

"Yes, I know, you loved her. I don't care if you did kill her. That is not my concern. My *only* concern is Miss Saxe. And from this moment forward, she is no longer accountable to you. You are not to meet with her in private without her lawyer—that would be me—present. You can talk about actual division business, but if your conversation goes beyond those parameters, we send the letter. If anything should happen to Miss Saxe, or me, the letter gets sent. Miss Saxe is free to leave this job, and you are not to contact her or threaten her or bully her. Is that understood?"

The director stood. "You think you scare me, boy? I can ruin you with one phone call to your boss. He and I go way back."

"I'm sure you could, and I'm prepared to lose my job over this. What I'm not prepared to do is to have any harm, physical or mental, come to my client. Is that understood?"

The director bristled. He unfolded his body to its full height, but he didn't tower over Israel.

"I'm sure if you had a knife or a rifle here, you'd give me a piece of your mind. My brother says you're a crack shot. Your reputation as a hunter is legendary. So, yes, I know what you're capable of. What people in this community don't know, but what everyone in the division knows, is that you were having an affair with Savannah Braddock and that you were the father of her unborn child. I would hate to have to reveal to your wife what a man of your stature and position was really like. This meeting is over. Going forward, if you want to contact Miss Saxe, you will go through me."

Israel offered his hand and helped me stand. I couldn't talk. I looked at the director helplessly, and he glared at me.

"You'll be sorry. This isn't over," he growled.

"Yes, I believe it is," Israel said calmly as he led me out of the office.

We passed the secretary's alcove, took the elevator down to the ground floor, and I was still shaking. He gathered me into his arms.

"I was useless in there. I couldn't even manage to speak."

"Merritt, you are the strongest woman I know. You had to go through this nightmare by yourself, and you held up like a trouper. Now, you're not alone. You have me."

"He was furious," I said, which was unnecessary since it had been so obvious. "He's not the type of man used to taking orders. You were fierce. Thank you."

"Believe me, I was shaking inside."

"I couldn't tell, the way you blasted in there and took charge."

"Take no prisoners." He laughed. "Get it?"

I laughed with him. "Yes, I get it. The director has enough prisoners already. And one of them will probably go down for murder. Did you mean what you said, that you didn't care whether or not he killed Savannah?"

"Yes. You are my first priority."

"I'm not sure I can go back to work."

Israel kissed me on the top of my head. "You are my brave girl. You *can* go back, and you will."

"He promoted me, and I don't deserve it."

"Well, then, go back in there and prove that you're more than just an alibi."

"I'm afraid he might retaliate."

"Well, I think we put the fear of God into him. He can rage all he wants. He's powerless. And, if you're worried, you're going to be staying with me until this mess is cleared up."

"What about my apartment?"

"I want you with me, Merritt. I'm terrified to let you out of my sight, but he's not going to do anything at work. And at night, you'll be with me, safe and sound."

I hugged him. "I don't know what I'd do without you."

"You're never going to have to find out. So, back into the lion's den you go, my angel, and here's my address. I want you to come straight home to me after work."

"Home?"

He hugged me. "Home."

With Israel on my side, I felt like I was part of a team. Together, we were stronger. I threw myself into my work, assisting Peggy and Stanley with the Tent City project. The director didn't darken our door all day, which was unusual. Typically, Peggy was burning a path to his door or he was out and about micromanaging things in our office.

"I heard you had a meeting with the director," Peggy asked. "How did it go? Did the Tent City project come up?"

"Nothing specific about that. I don't think we'll be working together anymore on that special project." Just repeating that phrase left a dark stain in my mind, a stain I couldn't wait to get home to wash off. Well, not at my apartment. My new, albeit temporary, home. Of course we would go back to my apartment together to gather up my things, but the thought of showering with my new roommate was a tempting prospect.

Peggy was beyond thrilled to have me back. "You did good work today," she said. "Hope everything is okay with your family."

I hadn't told her why I'd had to suddenly leave work, and they had given me my privacy, so the less said the better.

"Everything at home is fine," I assured her. "Thanks for asking."

I walked to my car, careful to look around for lurkers. I didn't know what my next step was. Would I quit and go back to Miami and get another job? Would I possibly accept Daniel's proposal? How long could I comfortably stay at Israel's place? What was our relationship, exactly? He'd told me he loved me, and I was falling more in love with him every day. But was he ready to commit? Was that even what I really wanted? Or was it just all about sex?

Chapter Twenty-Two

When I arrived at Israel's house, he opened the door and took me into his arms.

"Merritt," he breathed, pressing my body against his.

"I wasn't gone that long."

"A minute is too long to be without you," he said.

"Aren't you the romantic one tonight. Do you usually get home this early?"

"No, but I wanted to make you dinner." He released me and splayed his hand across his chest. "Exhibit A. Didn't you notice my apron?"

His apron was emblazoned with the words, "Kiss the Cook."

"You're cooking for me?"

"Yes, I'm not only romantic, I'm domestic."

"Good to know."

"Come in and take a look at your new home."

"When you said your place, I had no idea you lived in a house, and such a nice one."

"Why not? An apartment is too impermanent. I'm ready to settle down."

"Oh."

"When I find the right woman, which I think I have."

"Really?"

"But first, obey the apron and kiss me properly."

He kissed me until I was weak in the knees. It was all I could do to pry myself out of his grip.

"Your neighbors are going to complain."

"Then let's take this inside," he invited.

"You are in a strange mood tonight."

"It occurred to me that you don't really know my moods that well. That's all going to change. I want you to know everything about me, and I want to know everything about you."

"So shacking up would be your way of getting to know me?"

"Merritt, it's more than shacking up. I thought you knew that. It's more like protective custody. I'm your bodyguard, and I'm never going to let you go."

"Oooh, Counselor, that sounds mildly suggestive."

"There's nothing mild about it. If I didn't have my world-famous Goodspeed spaghetti sauce cooking on the stove, we'd begin our first lesson."

"I love spaghetti," I exclaimed.

"I know you love Italian food, so I am going to learn to make your favorite dishes."

Impulsively, I jumped back into his arms and wrapped my legs around his waist. "You are my favorite dish."

"Don't tempt me, you little vixen, or the spaghetti sauce will burn."

"Well, I'm burning for you now."

"In that case, let me take the sauce off the stove, and we'll heat things up in the bedroom."

Chapter Twenty-Three

That weekend, when we drove to my apartment to get more clothes, I opened the door—and screamed.

Israel rushed into the foyer behind me.

"What is it?"

"Israel, look! Someone broke into my apartment."

Drawers were opened and contents dumped. My papers and books were thrown from the bookshelf. I ran into my bedroom. My underwear drawers were ransacked. All the clothes in my closet were torn off the hangers and lay in a heap on the floor. There wasn't one spot in the apartment left untouched.

"That bastard," Israel swore. He walked over to the telephone and dialed his brother's number.

"Four, we need to talk. I'm at Merritt's, and someone broke into her place and trashed it. They were apparently looking for the letter she wrote or something she has that they want. We need to pay a visit to the director. Yes, now. It can't wait. He violated our agreement. This can't keep going on. Merritt is scared out of her mind. What if she had been there when they were here? I don't even want to think about it. And bring your rifle."

"Israel!" I exclaimed. "This isn't *Gunfight at the O.K. Corral*."

Israel placed his arms around me. "Everything will be okay. We need to call the police."

"We already know who did it."

"He's too smart to have done it himself. He had one of his minions do it, but it has his fingerprints all over it. Don't touch anything until the police get here and process the evidence. Can you determine if anything valuable was stolen?"

I looked around the bedroom. My jewelry was on the floor, but I didn't have any valuable pieces. I had left Daniel's engagement ring, the only piece of jewelry worth anything, with my mother. I knew what the director was after—the photo of him and Savannah together. But I had followed his instructions. I'd put it in a safe deposit box at the bank. Or maybe he thought I had a copy of the letter Israel had threatened to mail.

"Just my peace of mind."

"He's trying to frighten you. Don't let him. We're going to get him."

"Israel, he's too powerful and too connected, and he's always one step ahead of us."

Israel tried to calm me down, but he was more upset than I was. "He thinks he's won, but this fight is far from over. When we make our next move, he won't know what hit him."

The police arrived minutes later. Israel introduced himself and me.

"Nothing valuable appears to be stolen, but they were looking for something."

"Do you know what that was?" the police asked.

"No, but maybe they left some clues behind that can help us identify who did this," Israel suggested.

"We'll let you know. Meanwhile, miss, do you have a place to stay?"

"She does," Israel answered. I gave them my phone

number at work, and Israel provided his work and home phone.

The detective gave me his card and entered my apartment.

"Listen, I'm going to drop you off at my house," Israel said. "Once we determine my house hasn't been hit, and my friend arrives to stand guard outside, Four and I are going to pay the director a visit."

I put my arm on his elbow. "Israel, wait, that's too dangerous. He has an army behind him."

"And we have justice on our side. He isn't taking us seriously. It's time to teach him a lesson. I'm not afraid of him."

"I want to come with you."

"I don't want you involved."

"I'm already involved. You're acting like Mr. Macho Man and I'm the helpless Damsel in Distress. This is my fight."

"Honey, I don't know how the night is going to turn out. If you're there, I'll just worry about you. I won't be able to think clearly."

"And I'm not going to stay home while you put yourself in harm's way for me. I go where you go. We're a team. Isn't that what you told me?"

Israel frowned and rubbed his mouth. "I had no idea you were so stubborn."

I smiled. "It's one of my best qualities."

He helped me into the car. "You know how to use a rifle?"

"No, I hate guns."

"Well, I guess if we get into trouble, you can argue the director to death."

"You're not really going to shoot him, are you?

That's taking the law into your own hands."

"I'm not going there with that intention, but I do plan to come away with the truth, whatever it is."

Chapter Twenty-Four

When we pulled up to the ranch, the lights in the director's house were still on. DC-1 was parked in the driveway, so the director was home. The plan was for me to wait in the car while Israel and Four, armed to the teeth, went to the door to get the director.

The door cracked open, and Miss Julia stood there in her robe.

"Four, what are you doing here this late at night? And isn't this your brother? We met at the holiday party. I'm Willard's wife." She extended her hand.

"Miss Julia," Four acknowledged politely.

"Miss Julia, of course I remember you," said Israel. "It's nice to see you again."

"Sorry to bother you at this hour, ma'am, but we're here to pick up the director for the hunting trip."

"Willard never mentioned a hunting trip to me."

"Yes, this has been planned for a while. It must have slipped his mind. We're going to meet some of the guys at the lodge. Is the director around?"

"He's in his study. I'll go get him. Would you like to come in?"

"No, ma'am, we'll wait outside. We don't want to disturb you."

"Well, it was nice to see you both again."

Four and Israel tipped their white hats in deference to Miss Julia. The white hats were a nice touch, indicating they were the good guys. The cowboy boots completed the picture. And there was something different about Miss Julia. Somehow, in the moonlight, with her white hair tumbling down her back, in her nightclothes and without makeup, she looked less severe, more vulnerable, almost disarming. I could see why the director might have fallen in love with her.

A minute later, the director bounded from his study and stood at the door. "Four, what are you doin' here? I don't know anything about a huntin' trip." Then Israel came out of the shadows. The director stepped back. "What's this really about?"

"Like we told Miss Julia, just a hunting trip. All the boys are down at the lodge, waiting. It's a surprise."

"More like an ambush," the director grumbled. "You boys are playing with fire. And you're going to get burned."

"We need you to come along with us to answer some questions," Four insisted.

"I'm not goin' anywhere with you boys."

Miss Julia came up behind her husband.

"Willard, I packed you some clothes, and here's your rifle."

I almost bolted out of the car. I knew Miss Julia was a crack shot. This was not going according to plan. I flexed my fingers.

"Ma'am, the director won't be needing his rifle," explained Four. "We're going to be hunting antlered deer. We've got centerfire rifles and pistols, shotguns, muzzleloaders, crossbows, and bows down at the lodge. But thanks for packing him a bag. That will come in handy."

Miss Julia lowered the rifle. She kissed the director

on the lips long and hard. "You boys have fun now. I'll miss you, Willard."

"I hate to leave Miss Julia alone here. The girls are visiting their cousins in Jacksonville."

Something the director said triggered a memory about the morning of the murder, but I couldn't recall exactly what it was.

"Miss Julia looks like a woman who can take care of herself," Israel said, looking at the rifle. "And we have a lot of business to discuss, about that *special project*. You know the one, Director. We don't need to bother Miss Julia about it."

The director scowled. "No, we surely don't, boys." He bristled, but he took the bag from Miss Julia, gathered her in his arms, and kissed her again. Then he walked out the door, wedged between Four and Israel, into the night.

I was hiding in the front seat.

"What's up, boys?" the director asked.

As a precaution, Four grabbed the director's hands and cuffed them behind his back. He put up a hell of a struggle, but Israel managed to stuff him into the back seat, fastened his seatbelt, and got in next to him, angling the rifle at his head.

As Four pulled away, I popped up out of the front seat.

"What the hell is *she* doing here?"

'You need to show the lady more respect," Israel said. "Not another word until we get to our destination." I'd never seen the director show fear, but from the look on his face, he was rattled.

We pulled up to a large log cabin. I'd never been to a hunting lodge before, but Peggy had told stories about it. It was empty now, but Four led the director to the brown leather couch and jerked him down roughly while Israel started a fire. I sat in a club chair across from the director. Then Israel sat next to me, in a checkered wing chair. Four stood guard over us with his rifle.

"What am I doing here?" the director asked.

"You're on trial for murder," said Israel simply. "I'm the prosecutor, and Merritt here is the judge."

"You can't hold me here against my will."

"We can, and we will," said Four.

"I have to get to the office in the morning."

"We still have plenty of time."

"I'll have your job for this, Four."

"We'll see about that."

The director was spitting mad. He tried to get up again, and Four pushed him right back down and twisted his arms until the director cried out in pain.

Israel rose.

"You remember this place, don't you, Director? The way my brother tells it, you and the boys came here often. You brought Miss Savannah Braddock with you regularly. I believe the room you shared with your mistress was that one over there." Israel pointed, and the director sagged in his seat. "Isn't that right, Four?"

"The boys were so jealous when you spent all those hours alone in there with Miss Braddock," Four added, "with all the giggling and carrying on. She squealed like a stuck pig when you bagged her."

"You bastard," said the director, sweat pouring off his forehead. "It wasn't like that with Savannah. I was in love with her."

"Do you deny that you were carrying on with your

mistress while your wife, Miss Julia, was home with your daughters?" Israel continued.

The director wore a remorseful expression while Four stood over him menacingly.

"Now, it's not that we couldn't understand what you saw in Miss Braddock—*Judge* Braddock," Four began. "She was as pretty as a kitten, sexy and willing, much like all the other young girls you lured up here."

"That was before Savannah," the director protested. "Savannah was different."

"She was the hottest piece of ass in Watertown. Everyone wanted her, but you took her under your wing, so to speak, and arranged for her, a young lawyer not five years out of law school, to be elected to the second circuit court, way before she was ready and way ahead of the more qualified candidates waiting in line. But she was always ready for you, wasn't she, Director? She had other qualifications. Me and the boys were salivating outside while you were otherwise occupied. We could only imagine what was going on inside that bedroom. You liked it rough and hard, and Miss Julia couldn't satisfy you, isn't that the truth? Savannah Braddock was just the latest in a long line of women you cheated with. And my brother's girlfriend was going to be the next one on your list."

The director's calm demeanor was slipping. He was in full rage mode now. He fought his bonds to get up again, and Four tapped him with the rifle butt.

"Israel," I objected. "Tell him to stop. This isn't right."

"I'm going to kill you, Four."

"Like you killed your lover?"

"I told you, I didn't kill her."

"You haven't heard all the arguments yet, Merritt," Israel reasoned.

I was growing increasingly uncomfortable with the vulgar language and the violent tactics that were being exhibited. This confrontation was turning into an inquisition. Israel was a man I no longer recognized. I didn't like the side of him I was seeing.

"You're not making the rules here, Willard," Four interrupted. "We are. Israel, continue."

"Then one day, and it was bound to happen, the way you two went at it like rabbits, as I understand it, you knocked up your mistress. Now you were fucked. How could you explain this to your *wife*, to Miss Julia. You weren't ready to give up that fancy ranch and lifestyle, embarrass yourself in front of the community and your daughters, and stain your reputation, and hell, maybe you even had feelings for Miss Julia. So when Savannah Braddock told you she was pregnant, you had no choice. You had to kill her. Isn't that the way it happened?"

Tears were streaming from the director's eyes. I wished I had never asked to come along on this intervention/mock trial. I couldn't take much more of this. Maybe Israel's strategy was to push the director to his limits to get him to confess, but somewhere along the way he had crossed a boundary.

The director continued crying softly. I bit my lip. This was difficult to watch.

"Isn't it? Do you deny you got Savannah Braddock pregnant? Do you deny you took a kitchen knife and stabbed your mistress in the stomach, killing her and her unborn child? *Your* child? And from the autopsy report, it was a slow and painful death."

The director choked. "It was my fault. I am responsible."

"There, now we're getting somewhere," Israel said. "Why don't you tell us exactly how it happened."

The director spoke in a more subdued tone. "I deserve to be punished. But I did not kill Savannah. I loved her."

"One step forward, two steps back," Israel continued. "This is an excuse we've heard before. Then why, when Merritt Saxe answered your call for help, did she get to the scene and find you covered in the blood of your mistress? And why do you persist in blaming Roy Starnes, or some unnamed ex-convict or everybody else but yourself, as the guilty party?"

Four picked up a hot poker from the fireplace.

"Brother, I think it's time for more persuasive tactics."

"Stop," I cried, rising from my chair. "Leave him alone."

"Miss Saxe, this line of questioning isn't for the faint of heart," Four said. "Maybe you'd better go into the bedroom."

Israel looked at me through hooded eyes with a look of resignation. "Do you want to wait in another room, Merritt?"

"I won't watch while you torture him," I protested.

"It's up to the director what happens to him. If he tells us the truth, we won't have to resort to violence." Four approached the director with the fiery poker, moving it slowly up and down, trying to decide whether to brand his face or somewhere quite lower.

Vomit rose to my throat, and I felt myself slipping out of consciousness.

"Merritt," Israel said softly and caught me as I collapsed. I woke up in the darkness of a bedroom, covered with a quilt. I hadn't stopped anything. I could hear their muffled words and see the scene they were staging through the open door.

"Now, where were we?"

Four raised the poker and brought the hot metal dangerously close to the director's face.

"Okay. I'll tell you what happened," the director relented, jerking out of the way of the poker.

Four lowered the poker and placed it back on its stand next to the fireplace.

"We're listening," said Israel in a deadly calm voice.

"It was right after the barbecue, and everyone had gone home," the director began. "I decided not to put it off any longer. I was in love with Savannah, and when she told me she was carrying my child, I promised I would leave my wife and marry her. I told Miss Julia, and she was furious. She stormed through the house screaming and threatening me. 'You will never leave me. I will not allow it,' she said. 'I'll put a bullet through your head before I let that happen.'

"I said, 'Julia, be reasonable. I'm in love with Savannah and have been for years. She is having our child. I think it's best that I move out of the house.'

" 'Best for whom? Don't you think I know about your whore? I saw the way you looked at her at the barbecue. And my friends delight in telling me all about the way you carry on with your tramp all over town. You have humiliated me and brought your dirty business into our home. I've let you play around, and I never said anything, but there's no way I'm going to let that woman take you away from me and the girls. We're your family.'

"Miss Julia ran around the house like a madwoman, breaking dishes and smashing glass and waking the girls. She wasn't herself. I didn't blame her. She begged me not to leave her, but I stood firm. Then she said she was packing a bag and taking the girls to her parents' condo on Jacksonville Beach. Before she could leave the room, she collapsed. I caught her in my arms and placed her on the couch.

"When she came to, she asked me to drive the girls to her parents. I covered her with her favorite plaid wool blanket and settled her in. I owed her that much and more. Things mean a lot to Miss Julia. Her things are much more important to her than I am. Savannah's theory was that women go overboard decorating and accumulating because something is missing in their lives. I think she was right. And that is my fault.

"I called Savannah and told her that Miss Julia knew about us and to keep the door open and wait up for me no matter how late. That I was coming to stay with her. And that we would never be apart again. I went through the house, packing up everything I could. I wanted to be moved out by the time Miss Julia woke up."

"Then what happened?" Israel prompted.

"I drove the girls to Jacksonville and turned right around and drove as fast as I could back to Watertown. When I got to Savannah's apartment, the door was partially open, and the place was trashed. Picture frames were broken, clothes were strewn around the place, and Savannah was lying on the bed in a pool of her own blood. My heart stopped. At first, I was sure she was dead. How could she not be? But then she reached out her hand, and I took it between my palms. I remember how weak her pulse was and how cold her hands were. I wanted to warm them up.

" 'The baby, she's killed the baby,' Savannah said as life seeped out of her.

" 'Who killed the baby?' I asked, wanting to hold her body against mine, but the knife was in the way. I've never been so scared in my life. I wanted to call an ambulance, but then I thought about how it would look. I wanted to pull out the knife, but I thought that would make things worse. So I held her hand in mine, and with her last breath, she said, 'Miss Julia.'

"I was stunned. I tried to confirm what she was saying, to make sense of it, but she was already gone. For the longest time I just sat there, holding her hand, trying to soothe her, but she was gone. That's when I called Peggy to pick me up. But Peggy was out, and Merritt answered the phone. And you know the rest of the story."

"Are you saying that Miss Julia killed Savannah?" Israel asked.

The director hung his head and nodded. "When I got home, Miss Julia opened the door, and she fell into my arms. She confessed what she had done. She wasn't sorry. She said she'd do anything to keep me. So you see, I had to protect her. Because it was my fault."

"She said she waited outside Savannah's apartment and saw Roy Starnes leave. That's when she went in and confronted Savannah, and she repeated their conversation to me: 'You're nothing but a slut, entertaining men in your bedroom in the middle of the night. Does Willard know about this?'

" 'Roy just came by to drop off my scarf.'

"Miss Julia checked her watch. 'At two in the morning? What else did he come by for?'

" 'He told me how he felt about me.'

" 'Did he know you were pregnant with my husband's child?'

" 'Yes, and I told him Willi and I are in love. Roy offered to marry me. But of course I said no. Willi and I are going to be married.'

" 'Women like you think you can have it all. Any man you want. Well, you can't have my man. You can't destroy my family. I'm asking you to step away. You're a temptress; you're the devil. If you leave, Willard will come back to me. I know he will.'

"Miss Julia told me Savannah held her palm over her stomach and said, 'I can't. I'm sorry, but there's a baby now.'

"That's when Miss Julia started to attack Savannah, taking the picture of the two of us and smashing it on the floor, grabbing everything she could out of the drawers and the closet and throwing it on the floor. Savannah didn't have much. When Miss Julia got as far as the kitchen, that's when she grabbed a butcher knife and...stabbed Savannah.

"If I had just gotten there a little earlier, or if I hadn't taken the girls to their grandparents... Miss Julia sent me away on purpose so she could ambush Savannah."

I climbed out of the four-poster bed, came out into the living room, and stood before the director. "You told me Miss Julia had taken your daughters to Jacksonville, but when I dropped you off, she was at the door," I said. "That's what I was trying to remember."

"So your wife murdered Savannah Braddock in cold blood," Israel stated. "Unbelievable."

"I don't think she went there with the intention of killing anyone. If she had, she would have taken her shotgun. But she gets enraged easily, and she lost it with Savannah and picked up whatever weapon was handy. She thought she was defending her family."

Four sat on the edge of the club chair.

Israel collapsed on the couch. "So you're saying you really didn't kill Savannah Braddock?"

"If I had only gotten there sooner, I could have done something. I could have stopped my wife. I pushed her too far. It was all my fault. I'll never forgive myself."

"Christ, what do we do now?" Israel asked.

Four shrugged.

"What are you going to do with me?" asked the director.

Israel shook his head and expelled a breath. "Let's let him go," Israel decided, and started uncuffing the director's wrists.

"I think we should all forget this ever happened," Four said.

"What about Miss Julia?" I asked. "She committed murder. Israel, you're a lawyer. You can't just let her get away with it."

"Like the director said, she was driven to the edge trying to protect her family," Israel rationalized. "She was probably temporarily insane when she picked up that knife. Let's just keep this between the four of us and never speak of it again. Agreed?"

"Just leave the case unsolved?" I asked.

"I think that's best," Israel answered.

The director sighed in obvious relief and flexed his sore hands.

Four nodded, and I was in no position to disagree. How do I know what I would have done in Miss Julia's place if I saw my husband's baby growing in his mistress's belly? I might have gone a little crazy, too.

Four and Israel picked up their rifles.

"Let's go, Willard. We'll drop you at home. You're not going to hear anything from us, and I hope you'll respect that."

"Thank you," the director said.

I had a lot to think about. I couldn't go back to the division or see the director ever again, and I didn't know if I could forgive Israel or look at him the same way, after the way he'd conducted himself in this mock trial. I knew he was just trying to protect me, but he'd gone too far. I couldn't erase what I had seen.

We dropped the director off, and as Four drove the car away from his boss's house and toward Israel's residence, Israel put his arm around me. "Come on, baby, I think we need some rest."

"I can't stay here with you, Israel. Not yet, anyway. I need you to take me home."

"But your place is trashed. You can't stay there."

"They're not going to come back. I just need to get away."

"Away from me?"

"I need time to think." Tomorrow would be a busy day. I was going to turn in my resignation and try to get out of my lease and put Watertown in my rearview mirror.

Daniel was starting to look pretty tempting. I didn't have room for any more drama in my life. I wiggled my ring finger. It felt naked. I was going to take another serious look at my engagement ring. The six-hour drive back to Miami would give me plenty of time to think. I hoped Daniel hadn't returned to UVa, and we could talk, really talk, about our future.

Epilogue

I left the Swirl & Curl, a beauty boutique that had just opened in town, after a color, wash, cut, and blow dry. I wanted to look nice for my anniversary dinner. I had purchased a new cocktail dress and was looking forward to a wonderful celebration at the club.

I wondered if my husband had read the obituary. That's all anyone was talking about. The director was an experienced pilot. There was no rough weather at the time of the crash. No one could explain how the plane could have gone down.

I'd kept my word about never seeing the director again, and I'd kept his secret, although I admit I kept track of him in the news and on social media. From all accounts, he had turned into a faithful husband and a good father.

With my husband's position in the government—he had his eye on the governor's mansion, and I was determined to help him fulfill his ambitions—he would be expected to attend the director's funeral, but I wouldn't be by his side. I'd long ago reconciled my feelings about the murder and let it go.

I'd lost touch with Peggy, as well. The last time I'd seen her was at the gynecologist's office a few years after the murder. We shared a doctor.

"Peggy, how are you?" I was surprised at how happy I was to see my former mentor.

"Great."

"Are you still working at the Department of Corrections?" I didn't need to ask. I knew she was. I knew she had moved up the ranks to the top position. A position she richly deserved. And I knew she had been happy to see me go so she wouldn't have to share the director's attention. I also knew she had never married. She was still married to the job.

"Yes, and I hear you're heading up the new PR firm in town."

"That's right," I said. I'd found my niche and was enjoying the work, helping to promote the new businesses that were sprouting up all over Watertown. "Are you here for a checkup?"

"Yes, what about you?" Then she focused on my swelling belly. "Sorry, I guess it's obvious why you're here. When are you due?"

"Any minute. I'm having twins."

Peggy placed her hand on my belly like most women are compelled to do to pregnant women.

My first pregnancy, which played a huge part in my decision about what to do regarding my future, had happened soon after I left Watertown. Whether or not it was fate, I would never know. I did know that I was deliriously happy with the prospect of adding to my family.

I levered myself down on a chair next to Peggy, and we began reminiscing and eventually got to the most recent news.

"I was shocked to hear about the crash," Peggy said. "The director was such a careful pilot. And what a tragedy to lose Miss Julia, too. Are you going to the funeral?"

"No," I said.

The physician's assistant called out a name. "Merritt Goodspeed!"

"That's me. They're calling my name. I'd better go. It was nice seeing you again."

"You too. We should get together soon."

"I'd like that." But I knew I'd never get together with her again. In a matter of weeks, I'd be focused on babies and breastfeeding and all the blissful and stressful things that come with being a new mother. And my mind was a million miles away from the still unsolved Braddock murder.

Daniel Krantz had married a paralegal in his law office soon after he graduated law school. He was working hard to make partner at his firm, according to my mother, who occasionally ran into Daniel's mother. Still no children. His fear of commitment was legendary.

I hoisted myself up from the chair and waddled over to the door where the PA was standing. "How are you feeling today, Mrs. Goodspeed?"

"Ready to meet my girls."

Once I'd determined I was carrying Israel's baby, I went back to him. I had to. I wanted to. I'd returned Daniel's ring. I looked at the beautiful diamond now sparkling on my left hand. Israel and I had a short engagement and a big wedding, and we were deliriously happy.

I wouldn't say Watertown was my favorite place on the planet, and Israel and I had traveled the globe, but the truth was I loved Israel, and anywhere he and the children were was home. I realized it wasn't where you lived but who you lived with. It wasn't about someone's last name or their accent.

Love or lust or whatever magic brought together two disparate people who were meant for each other—it wasn't rational. What made one man acceptable but another "the one"? After I met Israel, I saw Watertown through different eyes. The homey hair salon, the delicious fried chicken served at the local diner, the darling bakery down the street, even if they didn't know how to make decent bagels. When you're in love, who needs bagels?

A word about the author…

Marilyn Baron writes humorous coming-of-*middle-age* women's fiction, historical romantic thrillers, suspense, and paranormal/fantasy. A public relations consultant in Atlanta, she's a PAN member of Romance Writers of America (RWA) and Georgia Romance Writers (GRW) and winner of the GRW 2009 Chapter Service Award and writing awards in single title, suspense romance, paranormal/fantasy, and novel with strong romantic elements. She is the 2017 Georgia Author of the Year Award Finalist in the Romance category for *Stumble Stones: A Novel.* She's also a member of the 2017-18 Roswell Reads Committee.

She graduated from the University of Florida in Gainesville, Florida, with a Bachelor of Science in Journalism (Public Relations sequence) and a minor in Creative Writing. Born in Miami, Florida, Marilyn lives in Roswell, Georgia, with her husband, and they have two daughters.

To find out more about Marilyn's books, please visit her website at http://www.marilynbaron.com.

www.ingramcontent.com/pod-product-compliance
Lightning Source LLC
Chambersburg PA
CBHW072135170626
46813CB00004BA/1576